AFTER THE RAIN

ELIZABETH JOHNS

Cover Design by Wilette Youkey
Edited by Tessa Shapcott
Historical consultant Heather King

ISBN-10: 0-9965754-6-4
ISBN-13: 978-0-9965754-6-1

For Karen, who insisted Yardley have his love child

CHAPTER 1

I regret to inform you, *mademoiselle,* that you must leave the school next week, at the end of the term. There are no more charitable monies left, and as you know, your mother's funds ran out. You must admit the school has been very gracious."

"*Oui, madame,*" Christelle answered. She kept her eyes downcast.

"I am very sorry, Christelle. I have kept you as long as I could, but the board feels you are old enough now to provide for yourself. I will draw up a list of potential employers for you to consider."

Christelle nodded in acquiescence. What choice did she have? Madame Thérèse was the only one who had ever shown her true kindness.

"I saved a trunk of your mother's effects for you," the headmistress said warily.

Christelle jerked her head up in surprise.

"We did not consider it appropriate to give to you at the time. Now, perhaps, it may be of use to you." The woman pointed towards an old dusty trunk with leather straps and brass tacks. She then left the room and the door shut with a click.

It had been six years since Christelle had been deposited on the doorstep of the Harriot School for Girls in Paris, the day her mother had left for England. Her mother had gone in search of someone following Monsieur Clement's death, but had never returned. She had perished in a horrible accident in London, Christelle had been told on the terrible day she had discovered she was an orphan.

Christelle would not miss the school. Due to her circumstances, she had been merely tolerated and, all these years later, there were still whispers about her mother's occupation. She was no fool. She knew exactly what her mother had done to survive after her English husband had abandoned her. She had married Monsieur Clement, who had taken her in when she was desperate and penniless. He had done her no favours.

Christelle might bear his name, but he had been no father to her. She looked nothing like him and he had no love for her. Her mother had kept her away from him as much as possible.

When the other girls had returned home for holidays, Christelle had been the one left behind with the teachers who had no family to visit. Instead of kindness or affection, she was treated more as a servant. She owed her place to charity, after all.

But where would she go now? What would she do? There were no respectable jobs open to a girl with no connections or references. Was she destined to follow in her mother's footsteps? Christelle knew what to do. One did not live with the most beautiful woman in Paris without observing and learning.

She knew she was beautiful too, for it was a source of scorn amongst her fellow students. But she had not her mother's confidence.

Christelle looked out from the tiny window, staring over the roofs to the Seine and the Cathedral of Notre Dame. It was a cold, dreary day, and it seemed to reflect the foreboding she felt about being cast into the streets with nothing to her name. Could they not have spared her with a spring eviction at least? A white pigeon landed in front of her on the window-sill, cocking its head around, looking lost.

She placed her hand slowly against the pane and the bird pecked at it.

"I have no food for you, little one," she said sadly. "Soon there will be no food for me if I cannot think of something quickly."

The bird flew away, and she turned and eyed the trunk warily.

It only took a few short steps in her tiny attic room to reach the familiar old chest of her mother's. She had thought all was lost of her. Christelle ran her hand lovingly through the dust that had settled on it to find the initials LAS. She traced the letters with her finger and wondered why she had never known anything of her mother's family. There had been no one to turn to when her mother died. But then, they had not planned for her to die so young.

She undid the buckled strap and slowly lifted the lid. Her nostrils were assailed by a mixture of cedar and her mother's fragrance of roses. Sadness threatened to overwhelm her as she picked up the garment in which she had last seen her mother alive. It was a bright jonquil silk, and she recalled quite vividly helping her mother put stitches into it. Her mother had been a gifted seamstress and had taught Christelle to sew as early as she could remember.

She began to rummage through her mother's beautiful gowns, and ideas of how she could rework them for her own use began to form. Perhaps they would be considered unsuitable for a young girl, but the dresses had been the height of fashion in Paris at the time. Christelle wondered if her own talents with needle and thread might be her only hope of survival for the near future.

At the bottom of the trunk she found some of her own possessions. One was a small stuffed doll she had carried everywhere as a child. She picked it up and held it to her cheek and tears of longing for her mother streamed down her cheeks. She squeezed the doll tight and felt something hard inside it. Pulling it away from her body, she begin to examine it. There had been nothing inside it when she was a child, she was certain. She found some tiny stitches that had been added to a seam.

She took a small pair of scissors from her sewing kit and cut open the new seam before digging through the stuffing for the object. When her fingers reached it, she pulled out what appeared to be a signet ring. It was made for a large man, fashioned of gold and with a black onyx at the centre of a crest.

Christelle had no idea who it belonged to. She had never seen it. Had her mother stolen it? Worse, had she received it as payment for her services? Christelle did not wish to think on it. However, she might need it to survive. She placed it safely back in the doll and re-stitched the seam.

Turning back to the trunk, she saw only a small leather journal at the bottom. She picked it up cautiously, unsure if she was ready to know its contents. She decided she would save it for later after she was resettled. She was placing it back in the trunk when a small yellowed piece of paper slipped out.

Christelle turned it over and read it.

Rosalind Christine Stanton
  Born the Fifth day of February, in the year eighteen hundred and ten,
  to Benedict Thomas Stanton and Lillian Adele Stanton

Christelle fell back on her haunches. "Is this me?"

～

Seamus Craig, formerly Douglas, had everything he had ever hoped for, and yet he wanted more. He wanted a wife.

And children. Several children.

He walked across St. James's Park and along the river towards Westminster, instead of taking the shorter route up the Mall. It was a cold, wet winter's day and the wind across the water found every minute hole in his greatcoat, but he sought the view to help him think.

He and his two sisters had been orphaned at a young age and had lived at the Alberfoyle Priory home. Whilst there, he had been befriended and mentored by a young physician, Gavin Craig. When

Gavin had unexpectedly become a baron, he had adopted Seamus and his two sisters as his own.

Seamus had gone on to become a physician too, studying at the Edinburgh School of Medicine, and had spent the past few years teaching in Sussex, at an academy created by Lady Easton.

He knew he was no typical bachelor. Most of the men he had gone to school with had little desire to settle down until it became necessary. But Seamus had spent much of his childhood longing to be part of a family again, such as he had known before his parents died. He had been almost finished with his schooling when Gavin had taken him and his sisters in and given them his name.

He had watched Lord and Lady Easton with their brood of children with some considerable envy. When he was at home, he'd observed Gavin and Margaux with their babes. He found great satisfaction in his work, and he had realized there would always be people in need and he would always be willing to help. Nevertheless, protracted hours in hospital did not erase his longing for a family of his own to come home to.

There was also a dearth of eligible females in Sussex.

The patients at Wyndham were almost exclusively male veterans, and there was little society in the country. Since Seamus also had a fascination with Dr. Withering's work on the circulatory system, and had studied with him, he had decided to try something rash and become a consulting physician.

He had talked the matter over with Lord and Lady Easton, and her ladyship had helped him arrange a post at the new Charing Cross Hospital in London, with one of her school's benefactors. Seamus had hoped his father would understand his decision. Lady Easton was all that was kind, and she assured him it was an excellent opportunity for him.

Seamus had packed his horse with his few belongings—his trunks to follow later—and set forth for the city. He had been to London before, of course, but he soon realized he was but a mere number amongst thousands. He found rooms in St. James's, not far from the hospital since he spent most of his time there.

Seamus stopped to purchase his usual meat pie from Mrs. Higgins. He was a creature of habit.

He quickly found a routine: eat, sleep, work. He neither knew where or how to begin looking for eligible females, so he concentrated on what he did know.

As each day passed, it was becoming more difficult to think of how to manage anything other than medicine. A physician's time was often not his own. He was, in short, a public servant. Hopefully, once he was established in his practice, there would be some semblance of normality—and time for the family he longed to have.

He was in a strange class, he thought to himself as he walked; a gentleman, and yet not privy to invitations on his own. He was not the type of person to draw attention to himself or put himself forward. The few bachelors he worked with were either too busy with their work to be troubled, or spent their evenings in gaming hells, chasing the type of woman one would not want for a wife. Perhaps if his adoptive parents were in town, he might meet some ladies at Society gatherings, but it would be some time before they arrived for the Opening of Parliament.

He would not give up hope, he told himself. His melancholy would subside when the weather improved. His situation was different from that of a country doctor; he had a small office next to the hospital, where patients came to see him. People were afraid of hospitals and the risk of contagion, but appeared willing to see him within this new arrangement.

Today was to be another long one of treating the infirm, and he already had a patient waiting for him in his office when he arrived. The man was sitting on the edge of his leather chair looking anxious.

"Good morning," Seamus glanced at his notes, "Mr. Baker. I am Dr. Craig. What seems to be troubling you today?"

"You look too young to be a physician," the man said as he looked Seamus over.

"I assure you, sir, I have been studying medicine since I was ten years of age."

"And what are you now?"

"Much older, sir," Seamus answered patiently. He had been through this kind of questioning before with older patients. Mr. Baker was a man of more than seventy and was apparently trying to avoid the purpose of his visit. Seamus knew how to go on. He waited for the man to speak.

"The missus made me come," Mr. Baker said after a lengthy silence.

"Ah, so you do not think you need to be here?"

"I did not say so," Mr. Baker said with a frown.

"Then how may I help you, sir?" Seamus leaned on the edge of his desk.

"It is my legs." Mr. Baker reluctantly pulled up the bottom of his trousers to reveal ankles the size of tree trunks.

"How long has this been happening?" Seamus touched the man's legs and the imprint of his fingers remained depressed into the ankles.

"A few months. It is worse in the evenings."

"I see." Seamus picked up his newest purchase from his desk. It was a new stick-like instrument from France called a stethoscope. "Do you find it difficult to breathe when you walk?" he asked, placing the instrument over Mr. Baker's lungs as he breathed.

"How did you know? I did not tell you," the man said with a suspicious look.

"I see your symptoms often."

"Then what is wrong with me?"

"Dropsy. It is a condition where the heart does not pump well and allows fluid to accumulate in the body."

The man appeared to contemplate the news for a moment. "I own a bakery and confectioner's shop on Bridge Road in Lambeth, behind Astley's. Me and the missus have worked there every day for five and thirty years."

Seamus was used to the older patients telling stories. He would eventually relate it to the diagnosis, he suspected. "Does your name have anything to do with your chosen profession?" He had to suppress a grin as he asked the question.

"Of course it does, young man. Are you being impertinent?"

"Perhaps a little," Seamus confessed. He was enjoying this, despite that the room beyond was likely full of waiting patients.

"That's all right, then. I appreciate an honest dealer."

"What is your favourite pastry to make?"

"Chocolate puffs. You won't find a tastier one anywhere in England." The man's chest swelled with pride.

"I will make a point to stop by and try one for myself."

"Then you had better make this dropsy go away. The missus will not let me in the kitchen again until it does."

Seamus wrote out a receipt on a piece of paper and handed it to Mr. Baker. "This should help your symptoms improve. You will need to reduce the time you are on your feet, and you must put them up on a stool several times a day."

"You seem to know what you are about, despite looking as if you belong in the nursery."

"I want you to return in one week to see how you are."

Mr. Baker grunted a dour assent before rising gingerly and hobbling from the room.

CHAPTER 2

*C*hristelle shivered as she stood in the pouring rain on the packet to Dover, despite being cramped between passengers. Madame had given her a week's worth of funds to live on, which was fortunate because she had been turned away from every position she had applied for in Paris. She had made a rash decision and purchased the passage to England.

She felt around her neck for the small string of pearls her mother had given her, hoping desperately she would not be forced to sell them in order to live. Her plan was to look for work as a modiste, but she could also cook and clean if she must.

Christelle had continued to have a nagging feeling that she should go to England and discover if she could find Benedict Stanton. Would he want her to find him?

She wanted to see him and then she would decide. Maybe he was a tyrant or a depraved person like Monsieur Clement. She would use caution, for she did not wish to be employed in the same way her mother had, or the other women residing in the house on Jersey where Christelle had lived for most of the time prior to her mother's death.

She had seen enough to know there would be no pot of gold at the end of the rainbow for her, and if she found her father she might not be welcomed with open arms. But she had nothing in Paris to keep her, and only possibilities in England, but she needed to see him. There were so many unanswered questions she had never thought to have answered. Was this man her mother's first husband? Christelle assumed so, but why had Lillian kept her father from her? Why had he abandoned them? Her mother had spoken little of her first husband and even less about the divorce.

She could always return to France if she hated England. Mr. Stanton was the only family she had—if he was even still alive. If nothing else, she felt compelled to see him once. She would think of what to say to him later.

The water was rough as they neared chalk cliffs, to which she could attest by the violent upheaval many of her fellow passengers were experiencing. Her serviceable brown boots were soiled and it was likely her dress was too. She said a silent prayer that she would find her way without too much difficulty. She spoke English well, but she was young and poor, and that did not get anyone far without an additional dose of good fortune.

Christelle observed the movements in the port as she waited for her trunk to be unloaded. Some passengers had family to meet them, and many others were heading up the hill towards the town. It was her best hope, since she could not afford to travel post to London. She would not make it far on foot, either, with her trunk being nearly as heavy as she was.

"Can I help you, miss?"

She looked up, startled. An immaculately-dressed man in a silver waistcoat, black coat and trousers was looking down at her with a kindly expression.

She had to remind herself to speak in English. "I am looking for the way to London."

"You may catch the stage at the Royal Hotel. Allow me to help you with your trunk."

"I am very much obliged to you, sir," she replied as he took her heavy burden from her.

"It is my pleasure. Where are you from? I cannot quite place the accent."

"Paris. I hoped I have no accent," she said, feeling shy.

"It is very slight, I assure you. I travel widely for the Foreign Office and am used to listening for the differences. I am heading back to the Continent myself, or I would see you to London."

"You have been very kind..." she said hesitantly. She neither knew his name, nor why he was helping her.

"Oh, forgive me! I suppose there is no one to introduce us. James Cole at your service." He removed his hat and performed a jovial bow.

"Mademoiselle Stanton," she said, trying out the feel of her new name on her tongue.

"That sounds like an English surname. Pleased to meet you, Miss Stanton. Wait here a moment," he said. He placed her trunk by her feet and strolled into the coaching inn, returning a few moments later. "The stage leaves at half past the hour. They are accustomed to timing departures with the packet arrivals."

"That is very convenient. Where may I purchase a ticket?" she asked.

"No need." He handed her one with a big smile.

"Oh, *monsieur*! I cannot! You must let me pay you," she said with astonishment.

"Consider it a gift to welcome you to England. I wish you well in London. Maybe I will have the good fortune to see you again one day."

"That would be very nice. Thank you so very much, Mr. Cole. I would be glad to repay your kindness in the future, if all goes well." She regretted the words the moment she said them. What if he took them for an invitation of the dishonourable kind?

"Do you have a direction?"

"Unfortunately, no. I hope to find work as a seamstress while I search for my family."

He paused for a moment with a contemplative look. "I would recommend going to Mayfair, then. The best shops are on Oxford Street and Bond Street."

"Oxford and Bond," she repeated so she would not forget.

"I had best be going," he said as a whistle blew the signal for the packet to return to France. He doffed his hat to her and walked away to the ship.

Christelle took a deep breath of briny sea air with a small feeling of hopefulness. "Let it be a good omen," she said to herself. Looking heavenward, she waited for her journey to begin as she watched the bustle of the passengers and ostlers changing teams of horses.

She began to stew as she sat inside the coach a few minutes later. She had no idea what the fares were, or how indebted she now was to Mr. Cole. But she could allow herself to panic and make herself ill, so she determined not to think about it. It was over and done with.

Christelle was also nervous about the new beginning. She tried to focus on the passing countryside and villages, but it was raining and dreary, and the poor roads with their deep ruts caused her to become overly familiar with her fellow travellers.

Several hours later, she was deposited from the crowded stage coach onto the doorstep of another coaching inn on a very busy street somewhere in London. At least she had had the reprieve of riding inside the coach, she thought, as she was pelted by the freezing rain. It was dark and very late.

She entered The White Bear to ask where to find rooms and was greeted with disapproving stares. The low-ceilinged room was crowded, warm, and bore the smells of ale and roasting meats. There was a bar filled with men and Christelle stepped forward bravely.

"Excuse me, sir. Have you a room for tonight?"

Several men looked up from their conversations and their tankards as the barkeeper looked around her.

"Where is your maid?" the innkeeper asked impatiently. Many of the stage passengers were also coming inside for assistance.

"I have no maid. I have only just arrived and have come to look for work."

"You had best try the workhouses across the river. Nobody will employ you around here without references," he said curtly.

"I have a letter from my headmistress," she replied with her chin up.

"That might do. You can try in the morning." He turned away to tend to someone else.

"Where may I find rooms tonight?" she asked to his back.

"A boarding house in St. Giles might take you alone. Ain't no reputable place going to take you here," he called over his shoulder.

Christelle gasped. She would freeze to death on the streets in this weather. Where was St. Giles? She could see she had reached the limits of the innkeeper's helpfulness, if one dared to call it such. She began to drag her trunk by the handle. It would not survive long with such treatment. However, she could not lift it for more than a few minutes at a time. She walked outside into the elements and looked around for another inn where she could try and find a bed for the night.

There was one across the street, which she thought another passenger had called Piccadilly. She said a prayer that she would receive more kindness, such as Mr. Cole had shown her in Dover. She picked up her trunk and struggled to make it across the cobblestones without being run over by the traffic.

The White Horse was about the same as The White Bear had been. The public room was full of men drinking and many stared at her when she walked in. She was too tired to care. She set her trunk down inside the door and looked for the innkeeper.

"Sir, do you have a room I may rent for tonight?"

The man looked her up and down. "I don't run that kind of place, miss."

"I beg your pardon?"

"Well, where is your maid or your chaperone?"

She hung her head. "I have none."

"Then I have no room."

"Can you tell me where to find one?"

"Covent Garden would take ye," he snorted out to guffaws from several of his patrons.

"I'll take you, sweetheart!" one man called across the room.

She ranted under her breath in French and dragged her trunk out of the door. Men could be disgusting pigs in all countries, apparently.

The publican did not run that kind of place, her right eye! He did not think she could pay.

Slowly she walked a few paces and asked the next person she saw for directions to St. Giles. He gave her a strange look but pointed the other way.

"Thank you, sir."

The man walked away, shaking his head.

Christelle began walking once more, lugging her trunk along behind her and picking it up to cross the road. After she had passed a few streets, she could no longer feel her fingers or toes. She looked up to discover a large bridge over the river in front of her. To the right, there was an imposing palace and church. Was this the right place? The first innkeeper had mentioned workhouses across the river. She had gone the wrong way.

The wind was noticeably fiercer and colder alongside the water. Tears began to stream down her face, partly from the wind and partly from the growing despair she felt. She refused to go to a workhouse. She knew precisely what that meant—she refused to sell her soul to one and die young.

She walked a few more feet on to the bridge and looked down into the water. Sobs shook her body and she began to consider the water to be more and more inviting. A conversation with herself ensued. Jumping was the coward's way out, and she was no coward. Surviving ill treatment at school and her mother's death were proof of that. However, she knew what the man at the inn had been referring to. Why was selling one's body the only alternative for a woman in her position? She was not afraid to toil hard, but first she had to find work. Leaning her arms against the bridge, she put her head down to shield it from the freezing wind and rain; she was too cold and tired to think rationally. Perhaps she could find a stable to sneak into for the night and everything would look better in the morning.

Suddenly she felt a body crash into her and she stumbled.

Seamus was whistling as he went along his usual route home from the hospital on this drizzly, foggy January evening. He was feeling unrealistically hopeful for an early spring, and he was becoming accustomed to city life. He was not yet certain he had done himself a favour by removing to London, but it had only been a few weeks which was too soon to pass judgement.

He looked across the bridge towards Lambeth and remembered Mr. Baker, the baker. He had not returned for his appointment that day. Perhaps he would try to find his way to the bakery on his next morning off.

He headed to the edge of the bridge to buy his evening meat pie from Mrs. Higgins on the corner, but hesitated and decided to keep going across the bridge to Lambeth instead. He had eaten too many meat pies since leaving Wyndham, which was not one of the finer points of bachelorhood.

It felt as though he had passed into the country, so different did the south side of the bridge look from the north of the river. There was a boat builder lining the bank, the large covered riding ring of Astley's Amphitheatre, and in the distance he even spied some windmills.

A few streets away, he found the bakery situated in between a greengrocer and a wax chandler, with rooms above for living. It was a neat establishment, the front windows displaying samples of its wares, surrounded by chequered green and white curtains to match the letters over the shop door. He immediately felt welcome as he opened the door to a bell's jingle. The delicious aroma of baking bread assailed him and his stomach rumbled in response.

An older woman, whose white hair showed around the edges of her mob-cap, smiled at him while looking over her spectacles.

"How may I help you, young man? We were about to close for the day, but I still have a few items for sale."

"I apologize for my lateness, Mrs. Baker. Do you happen to have any chocolate puffs left?"

"Why, no." She looked at him strangely. "How did you know my name? Have we met before?"

"I think not. I am your husband's physician, Seamus Craig. He did not keep his appointment today and I wanted to see how he was faring."

"Oh!" She scurried around from behind the counter and came to greet him. "You are such a dear to call on that old rogue." She walked to the door behind them and locked it. "Follow me, Doctor."

She walked through the kitchen to a set of stairs at the back of the building and began to climb slowly. Seamus was uncertain what he was walking into, but house calls were a normal part of his work.

"Raymond," she called.

"Eh?" the old man answered from an armchair near the fire.

"Your physician has come to see you. You failed to mention you had an appointment today," she said standing with her hands on her hips and looking down at her husband.

"It is not until Thursday," he said defensively.

"Today is Thursday!"

"It matters not." Seamus intervened before their exchange got out of hand. "How are you feeling?"

"Please have a seat, Dr. Craig," Mrs. Baker insisted before leaving the room.

Seamus pulled a chair up from the nearby table and sat close to Mr. Baker so he could examine him.

"I do feel better," the old man admitted. "My legs are less swollen and I can breathe easier."

"You have been using the foxglove?"

The dour man grunted assent. "And I have been putting my legs up on the foot stool after I work, as you can see."

"Excellent. Continue the medicine as prescribed and try to come and see me in about a month."

"I suppose I will receive a bill for your house call," he said in his gruff way. "I do not suppose you take payment in pastries."

Seamus had to grin at the old man. He started to leave when Mrs. Baker returned through the door with a tray.

"Where are you going, young man? You may not leave until you have eaten your fill."

Seamus promptly sat down again as though he were back in school. She had likely heard his stomach growl earlier.

He spent the next hour sampling some of the most delicious pastries, a mixture of savoury meat pies and sweet cream tarts—the best tea he had ever tasted—and being fussed over and coddled by Mrs. Baker. He discovered the couple had only had one child, who had died from a putrid throat before the age of five. They had been left to work in their bakery. He felt sad for them, as they were growing old alone, and this strengthened his desire to have a large family.

"I had best take my leave now, Mr. and Mrs. Baker. I must be back to work early in the morning," he said as he placed his cup in its saucer and stood.

"Yes, the day begins early for us as well. I will see you out," the woman said.

He followed her down the stairs to the shop entrance.

"Thank you for coming to see my husband, Dr. Craig. I knew you would be able to help him. He was able to make his chocolate puffs again for the first time yesterday. You are always very welcome here."

"Thank you, ma'am. I am just doing my job. Thank you for the tea."

She handed him a small box of pastries. "These were left after the shop closed today."

He did not object as he could tell it made her happy to give him something.

"If you insist."

She smiled at him with a twinkle in her eye. "Good night."

He could have hailed a hackney, but he preferred to walk, even though it was dark and rainy as it had been for most of the day. Night was his favourite time to see Westminster, the gaslights illuminating the bridge and medieval palace.

He began to rethink his decision to walk when the rain started to come down in small pellets that stung his skin. He pulled his collar up and his beaver hat down to shield his eyes from the sleet. He thrust his hands in his pockets and doggedly put one foot in front of the other, thinking about the fire and glass of brandy that awaited him in his rooms.

He was so distracted, he ran straight into someone in front of him.

"I beg your pardon!" he said, reaching out to steady the person from falling. "Are you hurt?"

The small figure shook its head, but continued looking down.

"Miss?" he guessed, although he had not seen the face. "Have I harmed you?"

"No. I am unharmed," he heard a feminine voice with a slight lilt say.

"Do you need help? Why are you standing on the bridge in this weather?" He was being intrusive, but his physician's instinct was warning him a body did not stand on a bridge in freezing temperatures for pleasure. "Miss?"

The woman finally looked up at him, her lids red-rimmed from crying. Seamus took in those large eyes staring helplessly up at him and his heart squeezed inside his chest. He could not walk away, much though his bones were growing weary and his feet were becoming numb. What of this little waif? How long had she been out here in the freezing rain?

"My name is Seamus Craig. May I escort you home?"

She shook her head violently and turned away towards the water. He blew out a frustrated breath.

"Miss, I cannot allow you to stay here and freeze to death."

"Je n'ai nulle part où aller!" she said with surprising spirit.

Seamus looked up in astonishment. He was not expecting French. He looked over her appearance and noticed she was dirty, but wore well-made clothes under her coat.

"If only Margaux were here," he muttered under his breath, wishing his half-French step-mother could intercede. His sisters had learned to speak more fluently than he had, since he had been away at school when Margaux came into their lives. He cleared his throat and tried.

"Je t'aiderai."

She looked up with wide eyes. *"Parlez vous Français?"*

"I am not certain I do. Let us find shelter from the cold and you can explain everything to me."

He began to lead her away, but she had stopped to pick up a trunk. He groaned to himself. She was either fresh from the boat or had been evicted. "Allow me."

"Have we far to go?" she asked innocently.

"Far enough," he replied as he walked to the end of the bridge and hailed a cab.

CHAPTER 3

*Y**ou are well served,* Seamus thought to himself as they climbed into the hack. He had wondered how he would meet a female, but this was not quite what he had had in mind.

"Where to, guv'nor?" the cabbie asked.

Seamus froze. He lived in a bachelor's apartment and it was frowned upon to take women there. Options ran through his mind—he could try his *grandmère,* Lady Ashbury, but he knew nothing about this person—except she was French, and that was not a good enough reason to impose on her ladyship late at night. He could not take her to Craig House and leave her alone. It was closed up and would not be ready for a guest. He had no alternative but to sneak her into his rooms for tonight.

"St. James's," he answered hesitantly.

Fortunately, his rooms were on the first floor and he could enter without a great deal of fuss.

He handed the girl down, paid the driver and unstrapped her trunk from the boot.

"We need to be quiet," he said to her and she followed him through the door. "These are bachelor rooms," he explained once they were inside.

A fire had been started and he was more grateful than usual for it. He removed his greatcoat and began to help the girl from where she stood inside the door.

"You are soaked through," he remarked, pulling back her hood as she stood there trembling. His breath caught in his throat when he took in all of her. She looked to be no older than his sisters and she was clearly frightened. He thought of how they would feel if they were in her situation. It could have easily been one of them just a few years ago. There was something vaguely familiar about her, but he could not place it.

"Come warm yourself by the fire," he said, guiding her shivering body nearer to the flames. She had not said a word since they left the bridge.

"What is your name?" he asked softly.

"Christelle," she answered cautiously.

"I will not harm you. I am a physician." As if somehow that assured her that all doctors were well intentioned. "I will try to help you find another place to stay tomorrow, but tonight I have no idea where else to take you. You may use my room for the night and I will sleep out here. Do you have dry clothes to change into?"

"If they kept dry in the trunk."

He carried her luggage into his bedroom. "I will call for some warm water. It is best if you stay in here while the servant comes." He turned to leave.

"Is that all?" she asked timidly, her voice shaking. "You do not wish me...to work for you?"

"Forgive me, my manners are lacking. You must be famished. I have some bread and pastry you are welcome to once you have changed." He was deliberately obtuse in answering her question. He knew what she was asking and his heart broke for her. What had she been put through already?

He closed the door and rang for the servant to bring some hot bricks and warm water. When the man had left, Seamus knocked gently on the door to the bedroom.

"Mademoiselle, the warm water is right outside the door, and there is some food when you are ready."

He walked over to his greatcoat and removed the now smashed pastries he had placed inside a pocket. He chuckled and put them on a plate. He was almost ashamed to serve them to this girl, but he suspected she was too hungry to care.

A few minutes later he heard the latch click and the door creaked open. Busy stoking the fire, from the corner of his eye he noticed Christelle look out of the bedroom, although she did not come into the parlour. When he looked up, he had to suppress an exclamation. She was clothed in a beautiful gown the colour of evening primrose, which highlighted her golden eyes even from across the room. Her hair had been brushed to a silky sheen and fell in long golden locks around her shoulders. Was this the same girl? He had to force his gaze away.

"There is food on the table. I apologize for its appearance. It did not withstand my pockets very well."

"Because of my trunk, I imagine," she said with a half-smile.

"Yes, I collect you are right. May I pour you a drink? I am afraid the selection is all bachelor fare."

"What is your choice?"

"Brandy."

"I would prefer it as well."

Seamus blinked twice, trying not to react. He should be astonished, but he was charmed. "Please, make yourself comfortable."

While he poured the drinks, he heard the creak of leather when she sat down in one of the chairs near the fireplace.

"Are you new to London?" he asked as he handed her the glass.

"Yes, I am just come from Paris."

He swirled the amber liquid around as he contemplated how much to ask her.

"I feel very silly admitting my story to a stranger, now that I find myself at your mercy," she said before he could ask anything.

"I will not judge you." He tried to be comforting. "I will try to help if you tell me how."

"I have spent the last six years thinking I was an orphan. Two weeks ago, I was asked to leave the school I was attending as a charity pupil. In my mother's effects I discovered I might have an English father."

"And you came here to find him?"

"*Oui*. All alone and with little money. I know it seems ridiculous, and even reckless, but I had nowhere to go in Paris either. I had no notion I would not be allowed to take a room without a maid. England has very strict proprieties."

"Mostly for young, pretty girls," he mused, then felt his face warm when he realized what he had said.

She did not seem to notice and kept speaking. "I had hoped to find work as a seamstress. I was advised to look for Oxford and Bond Streets, but I could not find a room for the night."

"They are all the crack in the *ton*," he agreed.

"The crack? The *ton*?"

"Forgive my cant. It means fashionable Society, or the *Beau Monde*. It is where the rich shop. You were advised correctly. Have you experience?"

"Most girls are taught to mend, but I helped my mother design and make her clothing before she died." She ran her fingers lovingly down the bodice of her dress. "This was the last dress I saw her in. We made it together."

"It is beautiful. I am certain someone would be happy to use your talents, but I have no knowledge of ladies' fashions." He had no idea where to begin, himself. Perhaps he could send a note to Lady Ashbury to see if she had a recommendation.

"Sir, I am grateful for your kindness. I do not know why you stopped to help me, but I also do not know what would have happened to me if you had not. I promise to leave early and be out of your way."

"There is no need to hurry. I can help make enquiries for you."

"You are too kind, sir. If you can but point me in the right direction, I know tomorrow will be a better day."

"I am certain you are exhausted. Have a good night's sleep and we can finish discussing this in the morning."

"*Oui.* I think sleep will be very welcome. *Bonne nuit, monsieur.*"

"*Bonne nuit, mademoiselle.*"

~

Sleep? How could she possibly sleep? She had been given a night's reprieve from disaster. Supposing this kind man had not helped her? She shuddered to think about it. Unfastening her gown, she stepped out of it before gingerly placing it over the chair. The masculine room in dark hues looked as though it had been taken over by a rainbow of femininity, she thought with the last ounce of humour she had left.

Christelle needed a plan. What if no one would give her employment? All of her gowns had been soaked through, save for this one. They were spread about on the carpet in front of the fire to dry. She had no idea if the others would be presentable when they dried without a great deal of work. She had hoped to show her gowns as samples of her abilities.

After climbing into the bed, she had intended to plot her next move, but the warm, thick blankets were too much for her weary body to resist.

Some noisy revellers awakened her when coming in from their evening entertainment, although she spied the dawn breaking through the curtains. She stretched and for a moment had to think where she was as she snuggled deeper under the luxurious coverlet and inhaled the musky male scent of it. She did not think she had ever slept more comfortably. Her thoughts ran to the *Monsieur* who had brought her here. How fortunate she was to have found someone who was kind! There were so many things that could have happened instead. They still could happen, she knew.

Seamus. Christelle had never heard such a name. Was it English? He had a slightly different accent from the other Englishmen she had encountered. When she had first seen the man, she had been terrified. He was tall and towered over her by at least a foot. But when she had looked up into his grey eyes, she had seen a gentleness which had made her trust him. Other men looked at her with unmasked lust, like those men in the pub. She had almost laughed aloud when she had come out of the bedroom, however. The look of astonishment—or was it relief—on his face had been a testament to how poorly she had looked before. It was a wonder he had helped her at all!

He was handsome himself, in a different way from other men she had known. He was intelligent and confident, although unassuming in manner. It would be easy to take advantage of him.

She shook away the thought. Her mother would have thought that way, but Christelle wanted to be different. However, she might do anything this man asked. *Non!* She jumped out of bed and began to dress. She must leave at once and not be a further imposition on his goodness.

She folded her few gowns as best she could and placed them into the trunk. How was she to drag it out of the apartment quietly?

Christelle unlatched the door, which opened with a slight creak and she froze. There was no movement in the room, so she opened the door all the way and turned to pick up the trunk. With a heavenward look and a heave, she managed to lift it. Turning sideways to hasten through the doorway was another matter. She bounced off the door's casement and stumbled. Still there was no movement. *The English sleep very soundly*, she mused.

Having struggled with the heavy object all the way across the apartment, she made it to the entrance and set it down to unlatch the door, when it opened.

"Good morning," he greeted.

"Oh, *monsieur*! You frightened me!"

"Were you leaving?" he asked when he took in her bonnet, cape and trunk.

She looked down at the tip of her boots peeking out from under her gown. "I had thought to, yes."

"I wish you would not," he said gently.

She looked up into his pleading eyes and would have given him her last penny. She could not recall anyone having been so considerate or generous to her before.

"At least allow me to find the name and location of some modistes for you. I have sent a letter to my *grandmère* to obtain a list of whom she patronizes."

"She is French, your *grandmère?*"

He inclined his head. "Let us sit down and drink some coffee. There are some things I could explain to you."

He placed a kettle on the fire and they sat in the leather armchairs around it.

"Please remove your cape and bonnet and stay for a while."

She did as he asked and looked up at him with curiosity.

He stared into the flames as he spoke. "I was born a gentleman, but my parents were killed in a carriage accident. My sisters and I were sent to an orphanage."

Christelle cast her eyes to his face. He was solemn, but he continued to look ahead.

"It was unlike most orphanages, thankfully. A viscount had turned one of his properties into a home and school. The physician who called on the school took an interest in me and allowed me to apprentice with him." Seamus smiled. "He took an interest in my sisters as well. When he inherited a barony, he gave us all his name and home."

"You know how I feel," she said softly.

His eyes met hers. "To some extent I do. I imagine it is harder for a young woman. When I saw you, I thought of my sisters being in your position."

"That is why you helped me," she stated.

"My step-mother is half French. Her mother is not truly my *grandmère*, though she insists she is. She is well-connected in Society and can perhaps help you find a position."

"I cannot impose in such a way!" Christelle had to fight back tears of emotion.

"Why ever not?" he asked with his eyebrows drawn together in a frown. "It is very difficult to find positions in England without a reference. I would not be where I am without help."

"But she does not know me or my talents. It would be asking too much of you!" she insisted.

He reached over and took her hand. She felt herself warm from the inside out.

"I want to do this."

Christelle looked up from their touching hands. His eyes were upon her, searching her face. She was not used to people wanting to help her. It was hard to accept. She hated being dependent on others.

"Please," he pleaded.

"*Merci*," she whispered. "I do not know how to thank you."

"If you succeed, it will be thanks enough."

CHAPTER 4

Seamus had been shocked to find Christelle trying to slip out when he returned. Did the poor girl not realize she would find herself back on the bridge or at a brothel within the week?

He had gone out to ask for a tray be sent up and had also requested his note to be delivered to Lady Ashbury. She was the most well-connected person he knew.

Seated at the small dining table, Christelle quietly ate the breakfast of bacon, eggs and toast he had shared with her while they waited for an answer from Ashbury House. It was not overly long in coming.

Seamus perused the contents.

Dear Seamus,

I wish you had told me you were in town earlier. You must come for dinner. As for your friend, Lady Ashbury is from home, but I can assure you Madame Monique is kept in business by our family! I will send a note and ask her to guide your friend in the right direction.

Stop by White's and have a dram with me this week.

Fondly,

Ashbury

Seamus looked up from the letter to see two golden eyes studying him.

"I am told a Madame Monique would be an excellent person to start with, and she will give you good advice. Shall I accompany you there?"

"If it would not inconvenience you greatly, I should be most grateful."

"Let me find a hack. If you are ready?"

"I am."

"Wait here, then, until I locate one."

A few minutes passed before Seamus was able to ensure the coast was clear after finding an available hackney carriage. Christelle had pulled her hood down over her hair and had wrapped her cape about her to hide her bright yellow dress. It seemed they made it into the vehicle unobserved except by a few tradesmen who were out and about early. He directed the driver to Madame Monique's and sat back in the corner, feeling nervous to be advocating on Christelle's behalf.

When they arrived and alighted, Christelle stopped and looked around her.

"Are you ready?" he asked.

"I think so. I am most anxious," she confessed.

He smiled to reassure her and opened the door. A little bell jingled as they stepped inside. Again, Christelle looked around, rather as a child would in a sweet shop, at the sample fabrics and gowns displayed about in an elegant salon.

"May I help you?" a middle-aged French woman asked. "It is very early, *non?*"

"Madame? My name is Seamus Craig. I was told you would be able to give my friend advice. She is looking for work as a seamstress. Lord..."

"*Mon Dieu!*" Christelle had turned towards Madame. The woman gasped and held her hands to her breast. Her interjection prevented Seamus from finishing the speech he had rehearsed.

"Is something amiss, Madame?" he asked. "I am a physician."

"*Non*," the woman said as she stared at Christelle. "Where did you find that dress?"

"It was my *maman's*," the girl replied timidly, looking scared. "We made it together."

"*Viens avec moi.*" Come with me.

The woman hurried away behind a curtain without waiting to see if they would follow. Christelle gave Seamus a questioning look but went after Madame. He did not know if he would be intruding or not, but he decided he would stay until she had secured a position and also passed behind the screen into the workroom. There several women and girls were buried in seemingly endless piles of fabrics, ribbons and lace. Madame proceeded with Christelle to another room off to the side, which appeared to be an office, and closed the door behind them.

The two began conversing rapidly in French and he could scarcely keep up.

I will hire you.

You must stay away from customers at all times.

I have a room upstairs you may live in with other seamstresses, as part of your pay.

Seamus was impressed by how quickly it all happened.

And he was a little sad. This little waif would be gone as soon as she had come.

With a start, he realized Madame was speaking to him.

"Can you have her trunk delivered here?"

"Oh, yes, of course."

"*Merci, monsieur.*" Christelle called to him as Madame turned her away and led her up a staircase.

Thus abandoned, Seamus exited the shop and walked slowly back to his rooms. *This is a good thing*, he told himself. He had wanted her to find work. He could not hide her in his rooms indefinitely.

He hailed another hack, loaded the trunk into it and took it back to the shop.

They used the rear entrance to deliver it, as suggested by the driver. Seamus had been hoping to catch another glimpse of Christelle. How else would he know if she was happy?

He sighed and went home. He lay down on his bed to rest, since he had scarcely slept, and could not stop thinking about the girl. Her jasmine scent lingered on his pillows and coverlet. It was much more pleasant than he would have thought. It only deepened his longing for more.

~

Christelle had to blink to fight away dizziness. Everything was happening so fast. She should be elated, but she had felt bereft when Dr. Craig had walked out of the door. She had not been able to properly thank him, and the thought of never seeing him again left her feeling as though she had lost a rock to cling to, which was ridiculous when she had not known him even four-and-twenty hours.

"Cheer up, *chérie*," Madame said. "I suspect you have not seen the last of him."

Christelle felt her face warm. Had her thoughts been so obvious? "He has been very kind and I did not properly thank him."

"Perhaps on your afternoon off you may visit him."

"But he lives in bachelor rooms. I could not call on him!"

"We will find a way. Let us get you situated and introduce you to the other girls. We will soon be busy with customers."

Madame showed her to a modest but well-appointed room, which held three single beds, one on each wall. It was painted in a soft lilac colour, and her bed had a pretty white coverlet that matched the curtains. It was clean and smelled of beeswax, which reminded her of her chores at school in a strange, comforting way. She almost felt as if she were back at Harriot. It also helped that Madame was French.

"You will be sharing this room with Noelle and Lorena. They are already downstairs, working."

"Very good, Madame."

"How did you meet Dr. Craig? Is he an old friend?" Madame asked as they descended.

Christelle debated how to answer. She knew the woman was fishing for information, but she did not wish to be dishonest when this person was giving her a chance.

"*Non*. He found me in the cold with nowhere to go and took pity on me."

"What an amazing coincidence," the modiste muttered quietly. "He belongs to a well-connected family. You are very fortunate indeed that you found one such as he."

"I am well aware of my good fortune. I had other offers which were more to my *maman's* preference than mine."

Madame looked at her, long and hard. Perhaps she had spoken too frankly. She loved her *maman*, but it would do no good to delude herself or anyone else. She was growing uncomfortable under the woman's scrutiny.

"You are not like your *maman*, I think."

Christelle shook her head to fight the tears filling her eyes.

"Do you share your mother's talents for design?" Madame Monique asked.

Christelle raised her head up. She had thought the woman had meant she was not like her mother in behaviour, but... "Did you know my *maman?*"

"*Oui*," she answered softly. "I knew Lillian."

"Did she work for you before the accident?"

Madame appeared to contemplate her answer for a moment. "I suppose you could say that. She sold me some designs."

"That is how you recognized me? I had not thought I favoured her to any great degree."

"*Oui*. She was wearing the same gown as you are now the first time I saw her. It is not something one forgets. I would be delighted if you possess the same flair for fashion she had."

"I would be happy to try, Madame. The dresses in Paris are quite different now. I would be pleased to draw them for you."

Christelle followed the seamstress to where some pattern books were displayed on a table in the salon, and wondered if her mother had made a similar impression in London as in Paris. Madame seemed to know.

"Are you here to make your living as a modiste? It is not easy to travel alone and begin a new life."

"It is more difficult than I thought. But I could not find work in Paris." She met Madame's knowing glance. She understood.

"I am most pleased you found me. I think everything will be as it should. These are our current patterns if you wish to look."

Christelle took some time to look through them and was satisfied. Madame led her back to a small table in her office.

"Now show me what you can create," she said, handing her some sketch paper and charcoal.

Christelle sat down to work and pondered all Madame had said. Was she willing to give her a chance because of her mother's talents, or despite them? She did not know... but she would do her best to keep the job through her own capabilities.

She was soon transported by her work and had drawn the six different dresses she had imagined during the time when she had been alone at school. Madame returned to see how she had done and began exclaiming excitedly.

"*Que magnifique!* I cannot wait to show these to the Duchess!"

"The Duchess?" Christelle asked with confusion.

"The Duchess of Yardley sets the fashion for the *ton*. Her Grace and her *maman* are my best customers." Madame laughed. "I would have hired you even if you had no talent, since you were recommended to me, but I am very much pleased that is not the case!" she declared as she perused the sketches.

"*Merci*, Madame." Was Dr. Craig so important she valued his opinion? Christelle was impressed.

"Please take a rest. You have worked very hard today. Your trunk has arrived and you will wish to unpack it."

"Madame?" Christelle asked quickly, for the woman was already hurrying away. "May I be permitted to buy some scraps and sew myself a gown or two? I have only a few of my mother's gowns and the plain dresses I wore at school."

"*Oui*, of course. I prefer my girls to dress well. I will see what I can find and send them to you." She smiled kindly before leaving to attend to the customers who were arriving.

Christelle climbed the staircase to her room where her trunk was waiting with a card. She smiled.

Mademoiselle,

I hope you can read English as well as you speak it. I am sorry we were unable to say goodbye properly. I hope you are happy with Madame Monique, but should you need anything or are ever in trouble, please do not hesitate to contact me. I have arranged with the porter at the milliner's shop next door to send messages to me. If you have a day off, I can take you driving—and if you wish to go—please let Joseph know.

Your obedient servant,

Seamus Craig

Christelle smiled and held the letter to her chest. It smelled like him. She was tempted to run down the stairs straight away and tell Joseph when her day off was.

CHAPTER 5

The next morning, on his way to the hospital, Seamus stopped at the milliner's shop to see if there was a message. The modiste's was closed, as it was Sunday, though he suspected there was still work being done. He knew Christelle was very likely still sleeping, but all the same he glanced up to where he imagined her rooms might be. He debated throwing stones at the window or even knocking on the door, but he did not wish to cause trouble for her. He knew some employers did not look favourably on gentleman callers and he did not want to sully her reputation. Disappointed, he walked away and returned to his rooms. He did not actually need to go to work today, after all.

He returned again on Monday morning, and Joseph, the porter, smiled widely at him. It was seven o'clock and the sun had not even risen. It was out of his way, but he had promised Christelle he would help her if needed, and he had to make certain he had not left her in an untenable situation.

He did not bother pretending to himself that he was not looking forward to seeing her exotic eyes and beautiful smile. It had been all he could think of since he had left her here the day before.

"Good morning, sir. You are about early! We don't see many gents afore noon!"

"I suppose doctors are not your typical gents," Seamus said with a smile.

"No, I suppose not."

"Have you any word from the young lady?"

"It just so happens I do. She told me she has Wednesday afternoons off and would be pleased to see you."

"Wednesday!" Seamus exclaimed. That only left two days to make arrangements.

"Yes, sir," Joseph said. "Do you have a reply?"

"Tell her I will call for her at four of the clock... and to leave messages here if anything changes."

"I will do that, sir."

Seamus handed Joseph a sovereign for his troubles and turned to leave. He stopped and looked back.

"Joseph, did she seem happy?"

"She was certainly smiling when she told me so, sir."

"Thank you. I will see you tomorrow."

Seamus felt relief wash over him. He had not realized how much he had been wanting her to say yes. Had she said yes because she wanted to see him, or because she felt obliged to do so? He frowned. Why must he ruin a happy moment with self-doubt?

Where should he take her? What amusement should he escort her to?

A drive in the park? It was exceedingly cold and he did not have a proper conveyance. As it was, he stabled his horse at his father's house.

A museum? Perhaps.

The theatre? It was not to everyone's taste.

He would ask her.

He walked with a spring in his step all the way to Villiers Street, whistling as he went.

Seamus arrived at the hospital without remembering walking there. He was to spend the day lecturing to a group of students about the heart and circulatory system. He hoped he would be able to concentrate. It would not do to bumble his first lecture at this school. Luckily, he had given this lecture before, at Edinburgh and at Wyndham.

He wondered what was in his diary for Wednesday. It would have to be rearranged. He wished he knew more about Christelle. He did not even know her surname!

Seamus thought his family would like her. It was a bit premature to think such thoughts, but it was true, nonetheless.

He stopped at his office to remove his greatcoat and leave his medical bag, when he saw Mr. Baker waiting for him outside the door.

"Good morning, Mr. Baker," he greeted the man. "What brings you here at this early hour?"

"The missus sent me, of course," Mr. Baker answered gruffly.

"Please come inside." He held open the door. "Are you having more problems?"

"I feel a burning sensation in my chest and as though I am going to retch. Sometimes the room starts spinning and everything is blurred yellow."

"Have you been taking the amount of foxglove as I prescribed?" Seamus enquired.

"I have," Mr. Baker said defensively. "I even took two doses sometimes."

"No, you must not do such a thing. Sir, you will kill yourself by doing so. You have toxic levels in your system. If you had continued, you would have very shortly been found dead."

"I did not know more was lethal. The apothecary always says to take another dose if I don't feel better."

"Unfortunately, not of this medicine. Stop the doses for a few days until the symptoms subside, then resume the precise amount I advised before."

"You don't have to bleed me?" the man asked with surprise.

"I do not think it is necessary at this time. If your symptoms worsen, we might need to take such measures."

The man looked relieved, even though Seamus had not minced his words. He had rarely found it useful to do so in medicine.

"Shall I call you a hack?"

"No, it will not be necessary. I had someone to bring me in their cart. The missus did not think I was capable on my own."

"Quite," Seamus agreed.

Mr. Baker grunted.

"I am glad you came to see me."

"The missus has been singing your praises all over Lambeth. Any poor soul who wanders into the shop has to hear about how you healed me. Next, she'll be hanging your portrait on the wall and renaming the bakery after you."

"Nonsense. Craig is not half so charming a name," Seamus quipped. "Tell her I appreciate the confidence and please give her my best wishes."

"She also wanted to know when you would come for tea."

"I will try soon, I promise."

Mr. Baker pulled an envelope from his coat pocket. "Here are some tickets to Astley's. The theatre is right next to us, you know. We thought you might be able to use them. She thought you might find some young lady to accompany. They are always giving us tickets, as if we were young," he muttered as he took his leave.

The old gentleman departed, leaving Seamus shaking his head. What if Mr. Baker had not returned to tell him he was having ill effects or had gone to the apothecary? There were quacks on every corner and no one to see that they did no harm. Hippocrates must be spinning in his grave, he thought.

The reason he was in London was to attempt to make medicine more of a legitimate science. He hoped to one day have evidence to support all practices in medicine, such as the use of foxglove for dropsy. Getting patients to follow instructions was another thing entirely, however.

He gathered his notes for his lecture and headed towards the auditorium with renewed zest to impart his knowledge to the next generation of students. He would not think about Christelle and their appointment together—at least not until after the lecture.

When he returned to his office from a long day of teaching to fetch his bag and greatcoat, his secretary was frantically pacing the office.

"Whatever is the matter, Mr. Melton?" he asked, feeling too tired for drama.

"Sir, you asked me to clear your diary for Wednesday afternoon."

"I did."

"It is impossible."

Seamus stared at him and waited for him to continue.

"Apparently everyone in town is desirous of seeing the new consulting physician for circulatory illnesses," he stated.

"I beg your pardon?" There were not five people in London who even knew what that meant.

"I have been taking appointments all day. It seems Lord Ashbury has spoken very highly of your skills, and now you are much sought after."

Seamus did not know whether to laugh or cry. Lord Ashbury meant well, but the last thing he wanted was to be at the beck and call of Society and all their imagined ailments.

"I will be happy to see whomever will come here for an appointment. However, I will not be available on Wednesday afternoons for the foreseeable future."

"But, sir!" the secretary pleaded.

"My mind is quite fixed on this. There will still be patients aplenty even if this displeases some others."

"Very well, sir." The secretary walked away with a disconcerted expression on his pinched features.

~

Christelle thought Wednesday would never come. It would be a nice respite from being inside all day, even though it was cold and raining most of the time. She was enjoying her work designing dresses, and the other girls in the shop were very kind to her. Many had been brought from France by Madame Monique and hoped to return to work in Paris one day, thence to open their own shops. It was the same dream many seamstresses had.

Madame was most insistent that Christelle not be seen, which seemed quite strange to her, since some of the other girls did fittings. Perhaps that was a service to be earned. Occasionally, she would peek through the curtain to stare at some of the grand ladies who patronized the shop. One day she hoped to see the elusive Duchess of Yardley. She was held in high esteem by all of the girls there and was spoken of as very beautiful. They also said she had two identical sisters!

Christelle wondered what it must be like to be a duchess. She had no grandiose ideas for herself, but it would be nice to have a family one day. She had never known what it was like to have brothers and sisters. Maybe that was why she was drawn to Dr. Craig. He had mentioned his sisters. He was very kind to her too. Some woman would be very fortunate indeed to have him for a husband.

Christelle knew she was not of the calibre to be a gentleman's wife. She had lived long enough at Harriot to know her station. Nevertheless, she could dream and enjoy Seamus's company while she had it. She suspected he felt obliged to make sure she was in a good position. That alone made him a hero in her eyes forever.

Christelle pricked her finger on her needle and immediately brought it to her mouth. Despite using thimbles, her fingers were unused to sewing constantly. They were tender and sore from frequent punctures. She had spent her evenings sewing herself a new day dress from one of her latest designs, and she wished to have it ready by today at four o'clock. There was just enough velvet for a bonnet to match, and Noelle had been kind enough to help her with it.

Christelle glanced at the clock: it was already a quarter past three! She slipped the rose-coloured wool gown over her head and Noelle helped her fasten it. She had made a matching pelisse out of velvet, with pleats and cording around the bottom. She quickly ran the brush through her hair.

"May I dress your hair?"

"Would you? *Merci*." She had never had anyone help her with anything since she was a child. It felt very nice to be pampered.

"Where does the *Monsieur* take you?"

"I do not know. Joseph did not say."

"The weather is not nice, so I would hope somewhere inside. Perhaps a museum?"

"Perhaps," she agreed.

"Are you nervous? I would be nervous. I have never been courted."

"Oh, he is not courting me!" Christelle exclaimed. "He is merely wanting to see how I go on here, I am certain. Besides, he is a gentleman. He would not wish to marry someone so far beneath him."

"Of course he would not," Noelle agreed. "But he could make you his mistress. It is the best you or I can hope for."

Christelle knew she was right, but it was depressing to hear. If that was correct, why had he not said so the first night?

"Do gentleman take time to make these decisions?"

"*Oui*! Sometimes it takes them months to decide. If they are to give you a place to live and nice jewels, it is not a simple decision."

Noelle placed the bonnet carefully over Christelle's coiffure and secured it. Christelle was filled with sadness and uncertain if she still wished to see the *Monsieur* if he was only wanting a mistress. She walked down the stairs to wait for him, and tried to tell herself that it was not certain those were his motives.

Dr. Craig arrived fifteen minutes early and smiled widely when he saw her. She immediately forgot her reservations and smiled back.

"You look very smart!" he said, not disguising his appreciation.

"*Merci*, I made it myself. Madame is very generous to give me the fabric."

"You are complete to a shade," he said appreciatively. "My sisters will be asking you to design gowns for them."

"I do not understand the phrases you use," she said with a laugh. "Does this mean you like the dress?"

"It does. It also means I need to mind my speech. I spend too much time in the company of bachelors. Are you ready to go?"

41

"*Oui*. Where are we going?"

"Astley's Amphitheatre, if you wish. Have you heard of it?"

"*Non*. I have not left here since I arrived."

"Do you like horses and tricks?"

"I think I would like them very much."

"Excellent. Shall we?" he asked as he held out his arm.

He escorted her into the waiting hack and they sat quietly next to each other. Christelle felt differently from the way she had the last time she had sat next to him.

The last time she had been worried about where her next meal would come from, and whether or not she would have a roof over her head the next day. She watched the buildings pass by. The rain had stopped for the moment and the world did not appear so gloomy on this occasion.

"How are you getting on at Madame Monique's?" Dr. Craig asked.

Christelle turned back to face him.

"Very well, thank you. It is better than I could have hoped for."

"I am relieved to hear it. I was afraid I had unknowingly thrown you into the lion's den."

"Not quite. It is hard work and many long hours, but she is also kind and generous with us."

"I wonder why more masters have not discovered they would have better employees if they treated them well. I would not care to be the type of master my servant might leave for dead in a dark alley if no one was looking."

"What a horrid thought! I confess, I have known masters such as you describe, though."

He smiled and tiny crinkles formed around his sparkling grey eyes. "You see? It pays to be kind to everyone."

"*Oui*."

"Are you hungry? Do you care for tea? I confess I was uncertain what you would like to do. The weather is not ideal for a walk in the park," he said, looking out at the cloudy sky.

"I think I would like that. I have been too nervous to eat today," she disclosed frankly.

Would that she could have captured the look on the *Monsieur's* face. It was a mixture of relief and pleasure mixed together.

"I wish all people possessed your candour," he replied.

"I know no other way. It is a blessing and a curse."

"The world would be a simpler place if everyone said what they meant."

"Perhaps, but pride often prevents us from saying what we ought."

"Indeed. I believe you are correct," he said after a moment's pause.

"I am unfortunate to know from experience," she added.

"You seem to have a good deal of it. You cannot be beyond twenty years."

"I am not." She did not wish to divulge her true age lest he think her a child. She had seen too much to go back to naïveté.

He did not enquire further.

"There is a bakery near the Amphitheatre where we may stop for tea."

"It sounds lovely," she remarked as the conveyance crossed over the Thames via the same bridge on which he had found her a few short days ago. How different she felt now—as though night had turned into day.

CHAPTER 6

Seamus was not sure it was a good idea to take Christelle to Mr. Baker's shop, but he knew they would be welcomed there. Mayfair did not boast any establishments where he could take a young lady without a chaperone.

When they had alighted from the carriage and paid the driver, he escorted Christelle to the bakery's door and held it open for her. The heavenly scent of sweet pastries and baking bread again overtook his senses and made his mouth water.

"Dr. Craig, is that you?" Mrs. Baker called from behind the counter.

"Yes, madam. May I introduce you to my friend, Miss... Christelle?" He did not know her surname! How embarrassing!

"This is Mrs. Baker and she serves a delicious tea."

"It is a pleasure to meet you, my dear. I am delighted you have come!"

"It is too early yet for Astley's and your husband invited me. I hope you do not mind my bringing a guest."

"Now, why would I mind? There is always food ready here," Mrs. Baker said with a grin. "Ramona, can you please watch the counter?"

she asked one of her workers as she untied her apron and placed it on a hook. "I am taking my guests upstairs for tea."

"Of course, madam," the girl said. She watched Christelle with curiosity.

Mrs. Baker led them up the staircase to their home above the shop. "I know you are really here to see how Raymond is doing, but I am always tickled to have company."

"We truly came for tea and company, but I am always happy to know how he does. I know you will send him to me when necessary."

"He goes on much better now, thanks to you. He had been getting worse and worse for years." She turned to Christelle. "I suppose you already know Dr. Craig is a brilliant physician, but my husband could barely walk or catch his breath before the Doctor helped him."

"I suspected as much," Christelle said with a kind smile.

"Where did you have that dress made, young lady? If I did not know better I would think it was from Paris! It looks straight from the pages of *La Belle Assemblée*."

Christelle blushed charmingly. "I made it myself, madam. I have but recently come from Paris."

"Ah, that explains it," Mrs. Baker said with a satisfied look. "Please have a seat, and I will find Raymond and put the kettle on."

When Mr. Baker had joined them and an array of sandwiches, tea and pastries had been set before them, Mrs. Baker asked Christelle questions which Seamus would far rather have listened to than to Mr. Baker.

It did not take long for Mrs. Baker to discover almost everything about Christelle. Seamus wished he had the same conversational skills. He had to listen with one ear to both exchanges.

She had spent her early childhood in Paris and then on the island of Jersey. Her mother had left her at a girls' school in Paris before coming on a trip to England to look for someone. Her mother was killed in an accident in London, and the school had kept her as a charity pupil these past six years.

"You poor dear," he heard Mrs. Baker say. It sounded eerily similar to his own story, Seamus reflected. He had had his sisters and Gavin to support him, however. While he noticed Christelle did not complain, it did not sound as though she had had the same goodwill at her own school.

"You are working at Madame Monique's? She is the most fashionable modiste in all of London!"

"Yes, I was very fortunate to find a position with her." Christelle looked towards Seamus with a shy smile.

"I know she saw a diamond in you. Just look at you! You could be attending any of London's fine drawing rooms in such a gown."

"Thank you, Madame."

"I suppose you had best go on to the theatre. You will enjoy it so. We are too old to go now, but it had the most fantastic tricks you will ever see!"

"Thank you for tea, Mrs. Baker," Seamus said as they stood to leave.

"You are most welcome. It is the most pleasant visit I have had in a long while. Do come again soon!"

The shop was bustling with people buying confections before the show began. Seamus felt mildly guilty, as he had not considered he would be imposing on Mrs. Baker's time.

They took their leave and began to walk around to the front entrance of Astley's Amphitheatre. It was a mixture of sights and sounds—and smells; a crowd of people intermingled with stables.

"May I ask your surname?" he enquired. He had been wondering about it since he had introduced her at the Bakers' shop and did not wish to be in the same predicament again.

She wrinkled her brow. "I am not certain what it is. I was brought up thinking my name was Clement, but my certificate of birth says Stanton. I do not wish to have the same name as that awful man."

Seamus had no idea who Clement was, or what his story was. It could not be good. Maybe one day she would tell him.

"Stanton is certainly an English name, and if you prefer it, then use it."

"Yes, I was thinking the same."

They found their box and watched the different classes in the audience as they waited. That was a show unto itself, especially the rowdy young bucks. There were several tiers of boxes around a central pit, and a large stage across one end. One box nearby held a working class family with seven children, and seated in the box next to them was a peer Seamus recognized although he could not quite recall his name. He was dreadful at remembering names. The man was with two young boys who were having difficulty containing their excitement. Seamus felt a longing inside for children of his own.

"Do you like children?" he asked Christelle as they watched the twosome, and their father struggling to make them behave.

"I do. I would very much like to have some of my own," she answered in her usual frank way.

He saw her make a quick face at the boys, eliciting a giggle.

"I always wished for brothers and sisters. There were many girls at school, but I never did quite fit in."

"I hope you find your happiness," he replied wistfully.

"I did not mean to say I am unhappy," she corrected.

"I understand. You can be grateful for what you have but still hope for more."

"Just so."

One of the boys began to cry, and the father kept looking around as if waiting for someone.

"May I?" Christelle leaned across to ask the man.

"By all means," he said with evident thankfulness. "His nurse is ill, and his mother has not returned from the retiring room." The little boy thought it was great fun to be hoisted over the rail to Christelle and Seamus's box by his father.

"Again!" he cried.

Christelle distracted him with the ribbons on her bonnet. Both Seamus and the man watched on with admiration.

"Have we met?" the man asked.

"You look familiar, but I cannot recall your name. I am Seamus Craig."

"My name is Roth." The man offered his hand to shake. "Are you kin of Gavin Craig?"

"I am his adopted son. I am now a consulting physician with Charing Cross Hospital."

"I have heard mention of you, come to think of it. It is a pleasure to make your acquaintance, sir." Lord Roth looked towards Christelle and cast a glance back at Seamus.

Seamus realized the man must think her his ladybird since he had not introduced her. And, of course, he had brought her without a chaperone. Why did protecting her reputation matter so much? He wasn't sure of the answer, but it did.

"May I introduce my friend, Miss Stanton? Her chaperone was taken ill just before we arrived and we sent her home. We had not thought it would be too scandalous in a busy theatre such as this." He hated making up a story, but he had to protect her.

Christelle acknowledged Lord Roth with a nod while continuing to entertain the boy.

"Ah, there is Lady Roth. Gertrude, may I introduce Dr. Seamus Craig, the son of Lord Craig, of whom I speak often, and Miss Stanton, who has entertained young Nigel whilst you were away."

When the Lady cast a questioning look at Christelle, her husband immediately continued, "Her poor duenna took ill on the way here."

"Are you any relation to the Stantons of Warwickshire?" Lady Roth asked.

"I do not believe so," Christelle answered softly.

"Miss Stanton is newly arrived from school in Paris," Seamus explained.

"Your toilette is extraordinary. Is this the latest fashion there?" the woman demanded of Christelle as she looked her over from head to toe.

"It is."

"You must take me there, Roth. I long for some new fashions," the lady stated with an affectation that annoyed Christelle greatly.

"I have shown the latest designs to Madame Monique. Are you familiar with her?"

"Indeed I am." Lady Roth smiled triumphantly as a horn sounded and the Master of Ceremonies began to shout for everyone to take their seats.

Nigel went willingly back to his box as the show began. Seamus then had difficulty taking his eyes from Christelle while she watched with a delight equal to that of the two boys seated beyond her. The performers did the most daring things—even Seamus was impressed. One rider stood on his head on a horse's back, and another stood with each foot on two horses! It was the most fun he had had in some time.

It was growing late when the show finished, and they both had to start work early the next day.

"Shall we find a place to have dinner? Or do you need to return?"

"I have eaten so much food tonight, between the tea and the treats here, it has quite made up for not eating earlier."

"Indeed, I am not hungry, myself. I shall escort you home, then." He held out his hand to hail a hackney. "Would you care to go to the park on your next day off?"

"I would like it very much, thank you."

Christelle said good night to Dr. Craig and unlocked the back door with the key Madame Monique had given her. She slipped off her boots and tiptoed quietly up the stairs. When she reached the bedchamber she shared with the other girls, she was surprised to find Lorena, Noelle and Madame waiting up for her.

"I was trying not to wake you!" she exclaimed.

"We could not sleep until we knew you were home safely," Madame replied.

"She always waits up for us," Noelle stated. "Besides, we wanted to hear how it went," she added with a giggle.

"He is very handsome," Lorena remarked. "And he is a gentleman."

"Sit down and tell us about it," Madame encouraged with a smile.

Christelle placed her half-boots under the bed, then untied the strings to her bonnet and unfastened her pelisse before setting them aside.

"Well, he was very kind as always. First, he took me to tea at the home of one of his patients. They own a bakery in Lambeth, next to Astley's Amphitheatre."

Noelle stood up and helped her to unfasten her gown and pull it over her head.

Christelle sat down on the bed and curled her feet up under her as Noelle began to take her hair down from its pins. "Then we went to Astley's. I have never seen anything like it! There were girls doing somersaults, riders upside down on the backs of horses, and animals doing tricks!"

"I have been there once," Lorena said. "I almost enjoyed watching the audience more than the performance."

"Yes, there were all types there," Christelle agreed. "There was a very nice family in the box next to ours, and the Lady wanted to know where my gown was from. I told her Paris, but that you had all of the latest designs here."

"Did you, now?" Madame asked looking amused. "Who was this woman with such good taste?"

"I believe her name was Lady Roth."

"I imagine she thought you were a lady, being with a gentleman."

"Or she thought me his paramour," Christelle said with a wry grin. "Although Dr. Craig told them my duenna had taken ill on the way there."

"He is one to keep, Christelle. He was concerned for your reputation."

"I am sure I do not know why. It seemed as though there were a thousand in attendance!"

"Besides, you are far too young to consider life as a courtesan. You have other options," Madame said kindly.

"How very romantic!" Noelle said dreamily.

"But I do not think he is mine to keep," Christelle told them sadly.

"Time will tell. Let us try to sleep now. Morning will come before we wish it. *Bonne nuit, mes filles.*"

"*Bonne nuit,* Madame."

Indeed, morning came much too early for Christelle. She had had difficulty falling asleep after her evening's excitement.

She splashed her face with cold water, dressed sluggishly and broke her fast with a roll before joining the girls in the workshop.

They all settled down to work on whichever gown they had been creating or embellishing the day before, Madame included. It would be another hour or so before the customers started to arrive.

"What brought you to England in the first place, Christelle? I have been meaning to ask you," Madame said.

"I was forced to leave my school in Paris. They did not want to offer me charity any longer, though I worked hard for them in return," she said softly. "Before I left, I was given my mother's trunk of belongings. I did not know it existed."

"How long ago did she die?" Noelle asked.

"It has been six years now."

"How nice to have some of her possessions, though," Noelle added.

"*Oui*, especially since it also contained my birth certificate. My mother was married to an Englishman many years ago, but they divorced."

"Was it his name on the certificate?" Madame asked.

"I am not sure," Christelle confessed. "But I came to England to see if I could find out."

"Perhaps I can help you find him, *ma fille*," Madame said as she went into the salon to prepare for a customer.

"What will you do if you find him?" Lorena asked.

"I do not know. If he is not a nice person, I think I will just leave well alone."

Christelle concentrated on her work, but looked up from the hem she was finishing when she heard the front doorbell jingle. She was tempted to look when she overheard Lorena say the new arrival was one of their best customers. Her ears stood to attention the moment she heard fluent French being spoken.

"It is Lady Ashbury," Lorena whispered.

"I hear you have a new seamstress. May I see her?" the lady was saying.

"Of course, very soon. She is occupied this afternoon," Madame replied.

Christelle frowned. Why would she say that? Was there something so wrong with her that Madame did not want anyone to see her? She had no idea why Lady Ashbury would even wish to see her.

"That is a shame," the Lady said. "I had hoped to see her before I went to see Margaux."

"Who is Margaux?" Christelle whispered over her shoulder to Noelle, who was also shamelessly craning her neck to listen.

"Another daughter."

"She is very talented. She has made me some sketches of the latest fashions from Paris, as well as some of her own designs. I had thought the Duchess might be interested," Madame said.

"*Oui.* Of course," Lady Ashbury replied. "May I see them?"

"One moment, please. I have been saving them."

Christelle hurried to the curtain to catch a glimpse of her ladyship while Madame went to the office for the sketches. Lady Ashbury's hair was like ebony and her skin porcelain. She did not look old enough to have grown children. She was indescribably beautiful. Oh, to see the Duchess!

Christelle had to pull herself away from the curtain before Madame returned. It was tempting to stay and watch. There were some people who drew you to them with their aura of mystery, and she did not want to take her eyes off Lady Ashbury.

To judge by the exclamations Christelle heard, the lady was very pleased with her drawings. Pride swelled in her chest and her eyes began to fill with tears. She hurriedly wiped them away so they would not stain the silk of the dress she was sewing.

"When may I arrange to meet this girl?" Lady Ashbury was asking.

"My lady, I am not certain that is wise."

Christelle jumped up and ran to the curtain to look. Why must she be hidden? She was tempted to show herself at once, but she knew she would lose her position if she did.

"Monique, I wish to meet her," her ladyship said in a calm, authoritative voice. "You must know I do."

Madame shook her head. "You must trust me. It is better this way."

"I do not understand. I do not appreciate secrets. If this is to save my family from a horrid scandal, you will do me no favours by delaying my knowing."

"Let me speak with the girl first."

"Very well. You will send word?"

"*Oui*," Madame whispered.

Christelle stepped back from the curtain as she heard the doorbell signalling Lady Ashbury's exit. What did it all mean? Why would the Lady wish to meet her? She could not stop tears from rolling down her face, nor could she move from the doorway. When Madame pushed back the curtain and stepped into the room, Christelle was still standing there. She stared at the modiste.

"What is wrong with me, Madame?"

Monique blew out a breath. "Come with me, child. There are some things you must know."

Christelle followed Madame upstairs while the girls watched. She felt as though she was being led to the guillotine.

CHAPTER 7

The next day, Seamus received an invitation to dine with
Lord Ashbury at White's Gentlemen's Club.

"More like a summons," he muttered to himself, tapping the note
against his fingertips.

After he had finished with his patients for the day, he went home
and changed into appropriate evening attire and walked the few
streets to White's. He was shown through the hall and into the
morning room, where Lord Ashbury was speaking with a group of
gentlemen, Lord Roth included.

That gentleman saw him first. "Good evening, Dr. Craig."

"Lord Roth. Gentlemen."

"Does your father join us in Town soon?" Lord Ashbury enquired.

"I know the entire family intend to arrive for the Season. My
youngest sister, you know."

"Maili will give everyone a run for their money," Lord Ashbury
said with a chuckle. "I cannot wait."

"Indeed she will," Seamus agreed.

"You have been spared thus far, Seamus. I had three girls at once!"

All of the gentleman made sympathetic groans and patted Ashbury
on the back.

"I must return home for dinner," Lord Roth said. "It was a pleasure to see you again, Dr. Craig."

The other gentlemen made their excuses and Seamus followed his step-grandfather into the dining room.

Once they were seated and served their brandy, Lord Ashbury looked thoughtful.

"Seamus, I asked you here because I wanted to see you, of course, but I also heard a rumour you took a young lady to Astley's."

"Lord Roth?"

"Yes, he mentioned he sat next to you and a beautiful young woman."

Seamus had to fight a blush. For goodness' sake, he was too old for blushing! He had done nothing wrong.

"I did."

"My boy, you will need to be more discreet. Your father and I are well-respected members of Society. If you mean to keep a ladybird, please do so quietly."

"Sir, Christelle is no ladybird. She is a friend."

"Is this the girl you found work for at Madame Monique's?"

"She is."

"You cannot court a seamstress, Seamus. You must see how the difference in your stations would make it impossible. She would not be accepted."

"I do not run in Society's circle, sir. I do not think people expect it of a physician."

"A very well-connected physician, Seamus. Look at your father, look at your uncle, the Duke, and even myself. I fully expect you to be a household name very soon. Take tonight, for example."

Seamus stared at his glass, thinking of what Lord Ashbury had said. "I think my father would expect me to be kind to her. I found her on Westminster Bridge, freezing to death after she arrived from Paris. I had to help her."

"Which is admirable. I myself would have expected nothing less. So now you feel an obligation to court her?"

"No." Seamus paused while the waiter placed the first course before them. "I did wish to ensure she was faring well at the modiste's shop, but I very much enjoyed her company. I strongly suspect she is a lady. She was schooled at one of the best learning establishments in Paris."

Lord Ashbury paused.

"If what you say is true, why did she come here alone and needing work?"

"She was orphaned. The school asked her to leave when she could not pay." Seamus stabbed his beefsteak, trying to control his anger when he thought of what she must have been through. He knew Lord Ashbury had a soft place in his heart for orphans. He even had a home for ruined girls in Scotland.

"It makes more sense to me now. I think you have done the right thing, Seamus. Perhaps we should make certain she has a maid to accompany her when you go out in public, for propriety's sake."

"I am not certain how to arrange that, sir."

"Lady Ashbury went to see how the girl goes on this morning. She will know what can be arranged."

"That is very good of you, sir."

"Lady Ashbury would have my hide if she knew I had done anything less."

After consuming most of their meal and the covers had been removed, Lord Ashbury swirled his glass of port and asked, "Why did this young girl choose to come to England? It is rather strange."

"She said she found her birth certificate. She thinks her father was English and wishes to look for him."

"How remarkable."

"Quite."

~

Christelle followed Madame Monique up the stairs to her room. Madame motioned for her to sit down, although she herself continued to stand silently for some time.

"You found your certificate of birth, *chérie*? Is that why you came here?" she asked gently.

"*Oui.*"

"May I see it?"

Christelle nodded and went to her trunk to pull the document out. She handed it over. Madame read the words before giving it back.

"Do you know my father? Is this why you hide me?"

Madame cleared her throat. "The good news is you do not appear to be illegitimate. I may know who your father is, but he is not why I wanted you hidden."

"Then why?"

"Because of your mother."

Christelle gasped. "What else do you know of my mother?"

"I think you are aware of what her occupation was in France."

Christelle inclined her head slightly.

"She caused great scandal here too when she was married. That is why she was divorced. But when she came back, it was worse."

Christelle had always believed it was not her *maman's* fault the divorce had taken place, though she did not know any details. Why else would her mother have given up a marriage and life of privilege? Admittedly, Christelle had not thought too much about the reason— but she had not known the man who was her father.

"I do not understand. How could it be worse? She was not married this time!" Christelle was confused.

"Lillian was working with Lord Dannon. Did you know him?"

Christelle wrinkled her face in disgust at the mention of the second most horrid man she knew, after Clement. Lord Dannon owned the estate on Jersey where Clement had sent her mother to work, and where she had spent most of her childhood. Dannon was not kind to the women there, and her mother had been afraid he would want Christelle.

"I can see that you did. Unfortunately, Lillian made some poor choices regarding him. Her death was caused by those poor choices," Madame said vaguely.

"I see," Christelle said quietly, sensing Madame was withholding some of the story to protect her. "I do not understand what it has to do with me finding my father. He was not Lord Dannon. I do not look like my *maman*, so who is to know?"

"Dear child, if only it could be so simple. Perhaps you should visit Lady Ashbury. I will send her a note."

Madame left, shaking her head and muttering, and Christelle was none the wiser as to what was wrong—except that her *maman's* past was following her, even here.

Within two hours, a carriage had been sent for her.

Madame came into the office where she was sketching some new designs on the small table beneath the window.

"Lady Ashbury has asked you to tea. I will help you change."

"Tea? All alone?"

"She is a kind woman and she can help you with the answers you seek. Now, what shall you wear?"

"I suppose I must wear the rose gown again. I have not had time to make another."

"*Oui, c'est parfait,*" Madame agreed as she helped Christelle to slip it on and fasten it.

"What shall I say to Lady Ashbury? Does she know who my father is?"

"You are not like your *maman*. Lady Ashbury is the person most able to help you, *chérie*. When she sees this, she will do all she can for you. Now take the paper you showed me and tell her what you know."

Christelle bit her lip to control its trembling as Madame fastened the bonnet atop her head and sent her on her way.

The carriage was the most luxurious she had ever seen. It was a beautiful white carriage drawn by white horses. The footman handed her inside and folded up the step. Christelle was afraid to touch the beautiful seat of ivory velvet and sat gingerly on its edge. As they pulled forward she had to steady herself.

They passed a few shops before turning onto a street with large mansions and manicured gardens. As the carriage pulled up in front of an enormous white stone townhouse, the footman opened the door and let down the step. When she climbed the stone stairs to the entrance, the door opened and a butler welcomed her.

"Mademoiselle Christelle?" he asked in a French accent.

"*Oui.*" She looked around in awe. Statues were in alcoves around the entrance hall, and the ceiling was painted with a mural of mortals and gods in deep hues of reds, yellows and blues. It was likely something from Greek mythology, but she did not have time to study it.

"Please follow me." He led her to a dramatic marble staircase, which continued up the entire height of the house. It looked like a palace!

She was shown into an enormous drawing room and asked to wait. The room was square with high ceilings. The walls were covered in a golden brocade with a fleur-de-lis pattern. The ceiling was decorated with intricate carvings, and the floor-length terrace doors were framed by silk draperies. Several sofas and tables were arranged around the room. A portrait of three identical beauties, who had to be the triplet daughters, hung over the mantle. Christelle was staring at it, fascinated, when the drawing room door opened and the butler announced, "Lady Ashbury, *mademoiselle.*"

Christelle turned, and the woman exclaimed, "*Mon Dieu!*"

The lady's face was white and Christelle was worried she would swoon. She ran to her side and led her to the nearest sofa to sit down.

"*Madame?* Are you all right?"

Lady Ashbury looked up with wonder on her face. "I do not believe it!"

"Shall I call for someone?" Christelle asked, wondering why the butler had not remained. He must have heard her exclamation.

"*Non.* I am not ill. I am in shock. I now see why Monique did not know what to do with you."

"I wish someone would explain what the matter with me is. It is most confusing!"

"I must speak to my daughter first," Lady Ashbury said, shaking her head.

"You know who I am?" Christelle asked with astonishment. "Yet, you will not tell me?" She began to pace back and forth across the elegant rug. How could this woman not help her?

"I believe I know who you are. I know who people will *think* you are."

Christelle stopped and stared at this woman. She wanted to scream, but tears began to well up instead.

"Oh, *ma chére enfant*," the lady said as she stood and put her arms around her. "*Je suis désolé.*"

"I want to understand," Christelle babbled, and Lady Ashbury took her turn in escorting her to the sofa. She pulled a handkerchief from her sleeve and began to dab away the tears from Christelle's face.

"You are an orphan?"

"*Oui.* My *maman* died in an accident in London six years ago. She had left me at a school in Paris before she came here. Two weeks ago they asked me to leave."

"Why did you come here, my dear? I suspect there was a good reason. It is not easy to travel here alone."

"*Non.* It was not easy. But you are correct, I did have a reason. I found this." She pulled out the document from her pocket and fingered it gingerly. Madame Monique had thought she should show her ladyship this. Christelle handed her the certificate.

"What is this?" Lady Ashbury asked as she took it and opened it. She sat there very quietly for a few minutes.

"Do you know who my father is?" Christelle dared to ask when she could no longer wait.

Lady Ashbury's eyes darted up and met hers. They held for a moment before she nodded.

"*Oui.* May I speak to him first? This will come as a shock. He has no idea of your existence, I am quite certain."

He did not know? It was a small comfort to think he might not have knowingly abandoned her, but Christelle would like to know who he was first. That had been her plan all along. What if she did not wish to know him?

"I do not know how I feel about this. Is he a good man, my father? I had hoped to keep finding him a secret," she confessed with a frown.

"*Ce ne sera pas possible, chérie*," Lady Ashbury whispered softly.

CHAPTER 8

*Y*our father has a family now. I am uncertain how this will affect him." Lady Ashbury's words rang over and over in Christelle's head as she travelled back to the shop. How would it affect *her*? She had a father. She might be able to meet him soon. He was here in England, possibly London! She swallowed hard. The carriage stopped in front of the modiste's shop and she was helped down. She walked in a daze through the front door and beheld the most beautiful woman she had ever seen. The woman had striking violet eyes and silky ebony hair, which was partially pulled up while allowing long curls to fall down around her shoulders. Her dress was of a light lavender wool, with a matching pelisse trimmed with a white braid. Christelle stopped and openly stared.

The woman turned and, on seeing her, shrieked as she lifted her hand to cover her mouth.

"*Madame?* Can I help you?"

"Who are you?" the woman demanded.

"I beg your pardon?" Christelle replied.

Madame Monique burst through the curtain from the other room. "Christelle, what are you doing in here?" she asked in French.

"Lady Ashbury's carriage dropped me at the front door. I left by the front door—I had not thought..."

"My mother? You have just come from my mother?" the stranger asked in obvious disbelief, though also speaking in French.

Christelle noticed there were other customers in the shop and they began to whisper to each other.

"Your Grace, may we go upstairs where we might discuss the situation in private?"

Monique began to escort the lady up to the sitting room. Christelle did not know whether to follow or not, but she crept quietly behind. This must be the Duchess everyone had spoken of, and she was more beautiful in person. Christelle was too confused with all of the possibilities that she could not begin to clarify what was happening.

The Duchess continued to speak to Monique in rapid French. "You and my mother are working together to hide my husband's bastard?"

Christelle gasped. Her father was a duke? Her mother had said she had been married to an important man.

"At first, I was not certain, though the likeness is quite remarkable."

"How could you, Monique? How could my mother? I do not believe this! How long have you known?" the Duchess asked, clearly incredulous, with her arms out and her voice straining.

"Only a few days, Your Grace. She arrived from Paris. Should I have left her to freeze to death in the cold?" Madame defended herself.

Christelle stood in the doorway, listening, tears streaming down her face. How could this woman, whom she had never met, say such things?

"Does my husband know?"

"I do not believe so, *madame*. Christelle knows very little. Her school in Paris asked her to leave when their charitable funds ran out. Her certificate of birth was in her mother's effects, which the school gave to her when she left. It was the first she knew of her father."

The Duchess sat in a chair and stared out of the window. She took a deep breath. "Who is her mother?"

"*Duchesse*, may I say she is nothing at all like..."

"Who is her mother?" she demanded.

"Lillian."

Christelle saw a flash of pain cross the Lady's face, and she could see her struggle to control her emotion. Had her mother done this woman ill?

"May I have a moment alone with...Christelle?" the Duchess asked after a few minutes' pause.

"*Oui, bien sûr*. But she knows very little," Madame repeated.

Madame gave Christelle a sympathetic look as she walked past her and quietly closed the door, leaving them alone.

"Please be seated," the Duchess said.

Christelle was terrified as she sat down. This was not at all how she had envisioned this happening. The woman studied her for some time and shook her head with what appeared to be disbelief.

"May I see the certificate?"

Christelle was shaking when she tried to fumble in her pocket for the document. She took a deep breath to calm herself before handing it to the Duchess. Christelle noticed the other woman's hands were trembling and she bit her lower lip while she studied the certificate.

"I must tell your father. How am I to tell him this?" she asked without looking at her.

Christelle could only imagine how this woman must hate her. "I am very sorry. I had not meant to hurt anyone. I did not know what else to do or where to go. And when I discovered I had a father here... I did not fully consider." Christelle knew she was rambling and her voice was thick with emotion.

The Duchess sighed loudly. "I do not blame you. I believe I would have done the same. Only, I do not know how your father will react. The circumstances with your mother were...difficult."

"Would it be best for me to leave? I do not wish to cause either of you pain."

The Duchess's eyes began to fill with tears. She reached forward and took Christelle's hand. "*Non*. We will deal with this. It is a great shock, to be sure, but your father will love you just as he loves his other children."

"I have siblings? I have always wished for siblings. Will you allow me to see them?"

The Duchess looked at her with sympathy in her eyes. "I think you must meet your father, first. I shall consider how to go about it. Do you wish to remain here until I can decide what to do? Or should I arrange for you to stay with my mother?"

"I think I would prefer to be here for now. Madame has been very kind, and I enjoy designing gowns."

"I look forward to seeing them soon. My name is Beaujolais. You may call me that if you wish. Until later, Christelle." The Duchess stood and left without looking back.

~

"I do not know what to do!" Beaujolais exclaimed to her mother as she paced the floor. "She looks just like him—and my own Rosalind. I could no more deny she is Benedict's child, than the sun rising in the east!" Her hands went up in exasperation.

"At least she does not look like Lillian," Lady Ashbury said sympathetically.

"Will I never be rid of that viper?" Beaujolais looked out of the mullioned window, but there were no answers to be found in the fountain or amongst the shrubs in the garden.

"Beaujolais, it is not the child's fault," her mother gently chastised.

"Of course it is not. I did not mean it that way. But Lillian deliberately kept the child from him—the poor girl, and poor Benedict. I do not wish to tell him. He will be angry!" She put her hand to her brow and closed her eyes. "I have no idea of the best way to do this."

"She appears to be nothing like Lillian, though time will tell. Monique said she thinks her mother died in an accident, but she did know Lillian had been a courtesan and seemed to be quite opposed to adopting the same profession."

"What has this girl had to see? Perhaps we should get to know her better before we expose the children to her," Beaujolais said thoughtfully.

"I can write an enquiry to Harriot's School, though Monique said the headmistress sent the highest recommendation with her."

"Lillian has been dead for six years now. One would hope her influence was minimized."

"And that she takes after her father," Beaujolais added.

"Indeed."

"How am I to tell him, *Maman*? And the entire family are to meet at Yardley in a fortnight."

"I think you should take her there," Lady Ashbury said without hesitation.

Beaujolais turned sharply to look at her mother. "I beg your pardon?"

"You cannot leave the daughter of a duke working at a modiste's! It will not be long until it is all over Town."

"*Mon Dieu*! She is the daughter of a duke! And of age!" It suddenly struck Beaujolais.

"It is best to take her to the country. She and Yardley need time to know one another away from prying eyes, and you can prepare her for Society."

"I do not know if I can do this, *Maman*."

"You can because you have to, *chérie*. You are a strong woman. Look at Margaux. She loves Seamus, Catriona and Maili as her own."

"But...Lillian!" No further explanation was needed. "And how will she feel when she finds out it was I who killed her mother?"

"It will be difficult. In time, she will need to know. You must try to welcome her and forget who her mother was. She is also Benedict's, and that is what matters."

Beaujolais nodded, though tears were spilling down her cheeks. Lady Ashbury stood and walked to her daughter to embrace her. Sometimes, it was simply best to cry.

～

"My father is a duke," Christelle whispered aloud to herself after the Duchess had left. She paced across the sitting room carpet and pulled at her sleeves. "My father is a duke. This is much worse than I imagined. What if he does not want me? The Duchess is afraid to tell him. Is he a mean man? Would I be better to leave?"

Christelle wished she had someone she could trust to talk to. She immediately thought of Dr. Craig, but she did not have a day off until Wednesday. She was so confused she desperately needed some time alone, but forced herself to go downstairs to the shop to complete her work.

Madame came into the workroom after she had dealt with her clients for the day. Christelle had one last sketch to finish before her work was complete. The other girls had departed an hour ago, but she had missed several hours today.

"How do you feel?" Madame asked.

"I feel very confused. I had not imagined my father would be a duke, nor why my *maman* never told me of him. And, the Duchess seemed very hurt. I do not wish to ruin their lives."

"Christelle, *chérie*. Lillian caused much difficulty for them, you must understand that. It does not mean you cannot know your father. He will want to know about you. I think he will be very shocked, if indeed he does not know of your existence. But in time he will accept you."

Christelle wrinkled her face. "It is not what I wanted to happen."

"What did you want?"

"It is difficult to say. I had thought to discover who he is and learn about him first."

"You are suspicious?" Madame asked with raised eyebrows.

"I suppose I am. My *maman* did not have good judgement about men."

Madame clicked her tongue. "It is sad you should have known such things as a child."

"I think she thought I would not realize. But I did. I could not help but hear things."

"*Oui*," Madame agreed sympathetically.

"Madame? May I ask to change my afternoon off? I wish to speak to someone."

"I think you will not be here long, Christelle. Your time is your own."

"Am I being let go?" She could not mask the pain in her voice. Where would she go?

"*Non.* But your father will not wish you to be here in the future. It is not seemly for the daughter of a duke to work. You are your own mistress, but may stay here as long as you need to for now."

"I wish to be here! It does not matter who my father is!"

"If only it were so simple. I think you will need some of these designs for yourself," Madame said as she looked over Christelle's shoulder at the sketch. "A lavender or light blue would suit you quite well, *non*? It will not do for you to have only one gown."

"But I have my *maman's toilettes.*"

"You shall not wear those, Christelle. Let Lillian's memory be put to rest with your new family. You carry the good of her inside you, but those dresses will only remind them of the hurt she caused."

Christelle shot to her feet and ran out of the back door. She needed some air. She knew her mother had done some immoral things, but they were behaving as if she had been a murderess or something equally horrid! Could she do this if she were to be forced never to acknowledge her mother's existence? But where could she go?

"Are you all right, miss?"

Christelle looked up to see Joseph standing before her.

"I-I think so. I have just had some news."

"Do you need me to send a note to Dr. Craig?" he asked with a concerned look.

She would very much like to see him, but did not wish to disturb him. He was a busy physician.

"I do not wish to bother him. I will see him on Wednesday," she said unconvincingly, even to her own ears.

Joseph leaned in closer and whispered, "He said if you were ever in trouble to send for him immediately."

"I am not in trouble, precisely, but I am in a fix which I need advice about."

"I will send him a note, but I will tell him it is not urgent. Will that do? He comes by every morning at seven o'clock sharp."

"Every morning?" she asked in wonder.

He gave her a big smile. "Every morning."

"Then please tell him I would like to see him soon."

"Yes, miss."

"*Merci*, Joseph."

He tipped his hat to her and she walked down the street and up again for some fresh air, wavering back and forth over what was best to do. It would be nice to know more about her father, the Duke, but she needed to be careful who she asked.

CHAPTER 9

*O*nly one more day until he could see her again, Seamus thought, as he finished the consultation with his last patient for the day. His diary had become increasingly busy over the past week, and filled with some notable clientele. He packed up his bag and pulled his greatcoat and hat from the hook on the wall.

"Have a good evening, Mr. Melton."

The secretary looked up from his desk. "Wait, Dr. Craig, I have a message for you."

"Oh?" Seamus immediately thought of Mr. Baker. Mr. Melton looked down at his notes.

"Someone named Joseph would like you to call in on your way home. He says it is not urgent, but important."

Was something wrong with Christelle?

"Thank you, Mr. Melton," Seamus called as he began to hurry from the office. He hailed a hack and instructed the driver to go to Madame Monique's.

He alighted as soon as the vehicle rolled to a halt, and went first to see Joseph.

"There you are, then," Joseph said when Seamus walked into the shop.

"Is something amiss?"

"I saw her looking troubled this afternoon, I did. So I asked if she needed you. I could tell she was wanting to say yes, but was not wishing to bother you."

"She did not say what was wrong?" Seamus frowned.

"No, she said she was in a... fix and needed advice." Joseph replied as if he was trying to remember her words exactly. "Then she said she would like me to send word to you, after all."

"Very good. Thank you, Joseph."

Seamus had no idea at all what could be wrong, but he went next door and wielded the knocker on the back entrance to Madame Monique's shop.

"Ah, Dr. Craig. You are here to see Christelle, I presume?" Madame Monique asked when she opened the door to him.

"Yes, if I may," he replied.

"One moment. She has just gone upstairs for the evening. If you will wait here."

Seamus worried about what could be wrong while he stood in the back room to the shop. 'In a fix' could mean any number of things. Supposing she did not want to stay here? What would he do then?

"Dr. Craig." Christelle greeted him with a look of relief on her face. "Thank you for coming so soon."

"Of course. Shall we take a walk?"

"Yes, it would be best."

He held open the door for her and they turned to walk down Oxford Street towards Hyde Park. They did not speak as they negotiated traffic and crowds, delaying until they had crossed onto the lawn. Seamus waited for her to begin her story when she was comfortable. He had learned early on in his practice to mostly listen and people would tell you when they were ready.

"I have discovered my father," she finally said. "Well, I met his wife by accident."

Seamus looked at her face. She was struggling to speak about it.

"That sounds quite uncomfortable."

"She was not pleased," Christelle agreed.

"How did she know you?" he asked, not masking the astonishment in his voice.

"Apparently I share a great deal of likeness to my father. Madame Monique had recognized me as well."

"He is a member of Society, then? Only the *ton* frequent her shop."

"*Oui*. His wife did not think he would be pleased. She thought I was his bastard."

"Your mother was married to him?"

"And divorced after I was born. I do not think he knows of my existence."

Or ignored it. Seamus kept the ungracious thought to himself. He hoped it was not the case.

"Is it not a good thing you have discovered him so soon? I had wondered how long it might take you to find him."

They walked down a pathway towards a small lake before she answered.

"I have not even had a chance to look. It was coincidence." A gaggle of geese walked over towards them, honking loudly.

"Do you have arrangements to meet him?" he asked as he steered them away from the birds.

"*Non*, and I am not sure I should," she said quietly.

"Have you changed your mind?" he asked, glancing at her face.

They walked a few paces in silence. "I had not considered... he has a family. He is a prominent member of Society. I..." Her voice cracked and she could not finish her thought.

"Christelle," he whispered and led her to a secluded area behind a copse of black mulberry trees. He had not expected this. "You must at least tell him. At least you are a legitimate child. It would be more difficult if you were not, but both of you deserve the chance to know one another."

She kept her head down and did not look up at him. What should he do? He wanted to take her in his arms and comfort her, but he did not wish to presume— until, that is, he heard a muffled cry and she leaned into him. He pulled her into his chest and could feel her trembling, and knew he had done the right thing. But what should he advise her to do?

He heard her inhale in rapid succession and knew she was fighting for composure. He never wanted to let her go. It felt so right to hold her.

"What if he did abandon me? What if he does not wish to know me? I think it would be unbearable." Her eyes were looking up at him, so innocent, so vulnerable. Yet all Seamus could think of was kissing her tear-stained face. She did not show any sign of moving away.

"You will always wonder about him if you do not at least meet him," he said, struggling to give her coherent advice when she was so close.

"What is the best way to find out about a person? I cannot walk up to strangers and ask what they think of him," she asked.

"I know very little myself. I could ask my grandparents, I suppose," Seamus said, though he could feel his face being drawn down towards hers. "You could try the daily newspapers, or ask Madame Monique. I imagine the modiste is a breeding ground for gossip."

"That is true," Christelle said breathlessly.

Was she feeling what he was? Or was she terrified of him? Her pupils were dark and wide, and her cheeks were flushed, which would indicate vasodilation. Pleasure, not fear. Before he could finish assessing her like any ordinary patient, she reached up and placed a kiss on his lips. *Have mercy*, he pleaded silently. Her sweet, innocent lips tasted of honey and mint. It was heady stuff, indeed. If only he could bottle the feeling and prescribe such for his patients.

When she finally pulled back, she was still looking at him so trustingly. What had he done?

"I should not..." he began. She placed her fingers over his lips.

"I kissed you. Do not apologize, or I will be angry. If you do not return my feelings, then I understand, but do not be the stuffy English gentleman about what was genuinely given."

He wanted to laugh at her choice of words and pull her back to show her how he truly felt. But he suspected she had too many emotions to deal with at the moment and could not think clearly about him. In all likelihood, she would have kissed anyone at that moment. But it was promising, nevertheless.

"Will you help me return to France if I decide it is best?"

"I promise to help you if you agree to meet your father first and give him a chance." And if Seamus could not talk her into staying with *him*.

"Thank you, for coming. I did not feel I should say these things to Madame."

"I am glad you trust me with your confidence."

"I do trust you. You did not take advantage of me when you could have done. I know you are a good man."

He hoped her trust in him was well placed. Now he realized he certainly should not have allowed the kiss to happen.

"I should return home. Will I still see you on Wednesday?"

He held out his arm to escort her back, and she took it and clung to him. It felt right, and he wanted her to stay there forever.

"You shall see me every Wednesday if you wish. Well, except for when I go to a house party in two weeks' time. My family will be visiting my aunt."

"How long will you be gone?" she asked, looking up at him with an adorable little crease on her forehead. He reached down and smoothed it out.

"Not long. I have patients to see here. It is not always convenient being a gentleman who works."

"I am thankful for selfish reasons. I do not wish you to be gone long," she said with the hint of a pout on her lips.

"Will you send word through Joseph if you are to leave? I would not wish your father to whisk you away and leave me in the dark. Will you at least say goodbye?"

"*Non.* I will never say goodbye to you."

Seamus hoped that was true. He was beginning to think this little lady might be the one he could spend the rest of his life with, if she were agreeable. Her birth did not matter overmuch to him, but it would certainly be easier if she were from the same class, regardless of her time as a seamstress. He left her at the modiste's entrance and felt cold and empty inside when she had closed the door. Perhaps he could ask his *grandmère* if she could accompany them to Yardley for the family holiday.

～

"Christelle, Lady Roth is here, asking for some of the latest designs from Paris. Do you have anything particularly suited to her?" Madame asked as she came into the sewing room the next morning.

Christelle held the charcoal up to her mouth as she tried to recall the woman from Astley's and her colouring.

"Perhaps she would benefit from a fuller skirt and a higher bodice —something of the military style, to disguise her height and long neck, *non*?" She drew a quick sketch on the paper before her and showed it to Madame.

"*Oui*, this will do nicely. What shall I do when you leave me? I have become quite accustomed to having you here!" Madame scurried back into the customer's salon where Lady Roth was waiting.

She would miss this if she had to leave, Christelle thought. Perhaps she could make an arrangement with Madame so she did not have to stop designing.

"This came for you," Madame said when she returned. She handed Christelle a letter.

"Was Lady Roth pleased?" Christelle asked as she debated breaking the seal or waiting until she was alone.

"She was. She ordered it and asked for another design. Well, open it!" Madame said impatiently.

Christelle slipped a finger under the fold.

My Dearest Christelle,

We would very much like it if you could accompany us to Yardley for a holiday. It will be best for you to meet your father in a restful place and have time to get to know the family away from Society. I would like you to remove here to Ashbury Place first, and I can instruct you on English ways. Please

*have Monique see to your wardrobe, and I will send a carriage for you on
Wednesday at two.*

Affectionately,
Lady Ashbury

"Not Wednesday!" Christelle exclaimed.

"What does she say?" Madame asked. Christelle handed the letter
over for her to read. "I knew you would need more clothes. We must
go quickly now. Do you have any particular designs for yourself?"

"I do not wish to meet him on these terms."

"Why ever not? Lady Ashbury is correct. It will be more appropriate to meet in the country."

"But what if it goes very badly? I will be stuck there with no way
out. I cannot ride away on a horse and escape!"

"From what I hear, you could get lost in the house and never be
found. Yardley is too civilized to treat you ill."

"I had wanted to ask you what he was like. Is he kind?"

Madame paused to think before answering. Christelle watched the
consideration in the expressions on her face.

"I would not describe him as kind, exactly, but he is a good man.
You do not need to fear him or that he will hurt you."

"Do you know him well?" she asked with open curiosity.

"He has been in the shop a few times with the Duchess. He cares
very much for those he loves."

"And those he does not?"

"I could not say. I would not wish to cross him."

"As my *maman* did?" Christelle asked without expecting an answer,
but Madame nodded slightly.

"Christelle, you are a lovely girl. Once your father gets to know
you, he will adore you. Spend time with him and allow him to know
you. Give him a chance."

"You make it sound so simple," she said in disbelief.

"*Non.* It will not be simple at all, but I do think when he knows
you, he will care for you as I have come to do in a very short time."

75

"That is very kind, Madame. Is there any special interest my father has? Perhaps there is something common we may discuss."

"Unfortunately, I do not know so much. But I do know he and the Duchess are passionate about horses."

"Horses? But *I* know nothing about them!"

"Then ask him to teach you. I will let you know a little secret about men, *chérie*. If you can get them to talk about something they love, they will think you are the greatest conversationalist that ever lived. And all you must do is listen!"

Christelle laughed. "Is it really so simple?"

"Usually it is. Women can be the same. If you notice I talk very little to the customers. Usually they know what they want before they arrive here. Of course, if it would make me look bad I will strongly recommend something different!"

"I need a book on horses," Christelle remarked worriedly.

"*Non.* What you need are more gowns. Come. Let us see what we can make for you in two days!"

CHAPTER 10

*C*hristelle packed her things—including the three new gowns they had managed to finish in two days with everyone working on them, other commissions having been put to the side. Madame had promised to send more when they could. Christelle wrote a short note to Dr. Craig and left it with Joseph. She could not imagine never seeing him again, but she wanted to leave him a proper missive just in case.

Dearest Doctor Craig,

I have accepted the invitation to meet my father at his country estate. I am to be taken there by my grandmère. I am most sorry to miss one of our Wednesdays, but I think this is what you would wish for me to do. I do hope to see you again when I return. If this does not work out for the best, please know you have my eternal gratitude.

Affectionately yours,

C.S.

She sealed the letter and asked Joseph to deliver it to Dr. Craig the next time he passed this way. She said goodbye to Lorena and Noelle, then waited for the carriage.

"You will be perfect, Christelle," Madame said. "You were very brave in coming here to find him. That was much harder than this will be."

"I wish I had your confidence," Christelle said doubtfully.

"You do. In here." Madame pointed to her chest.

"And if he denies me?" Christelle asked dubiously.

"At least you will not wonder any longer. And you always have a place waiting here for you here," Madame assured her.

"I do not think it would serve you well unless you hid me. But I do appreciate your kindness in saying so." Christelle smiled sweetly.

Madame kissed each of her cheeks. "You also have a handsome doctor waiting for you."

"A possibility, perhaps," she jested with a knowing grin. "*Au revoir*, Madame."

Christelle was assisted into the carriage by a footman in white livery. She had never thought white to be practical, as she had spent so much time on her hands and knees doing chores. Madame had insisted some of her gowns should be fashioned in white. While they were very beautiful, Christelle did not think they were wise choices.

Again, the ride to Ashbury Place was very short and she was soon being handed down from the conveyance. She could not yet believe she was to stay here as she stood looking upwards at the massive stone mansion trying to quell her fears. She climbed the steps slowly. Armand greeted her jovially as he had before.

"Welcome, *Mademoiselle* Christelle. I am to show you to Lady Ashbury's sitting room. You will be in the jonquil bedroom, and Sybil, your new abigail, will see to your belongings."

"*Non!*" Christelle objected strongly. "I wish to unpack my own trunk."

Armand frowned. He was not used to being questioned or disagreed with, but he was not pretentious. It was also not his place to tell one of the family how to behave. "She will not harm your possessions, *mademoiselle*, I assure you."

"I am used to doing for myself. I prefer my privacy."

"I will tell Sybil to wait."

They climbed two sets of stairs around the grand marble staircase before he opened a door into a beautiful light blue boudoir. It smelled fresh and fragrant, as it was adorned with vases of lilacs. The sun was shining in brightly and made the room seem heavenly.

"Ah, Christelle!" Lady Ashbury said before Armand had a chance to announce her. "You are very welcome," she continued. Standing, she greeted her with a warm smile and outstretched arms before Christelle could curtsy. "May I introduce Lord Ashbury? We have been waiting for your arrival."

A handsome man with silver hair and striking green eyes also rose from his chair and whistled under his breath. He held out his hand and took hers in a warm clasp. His eyes met hers for a moment and then he bent to kiss her hand. "You are very welcome, Christelle."

He turned to his wife. "I can see why the uproar, certainly."

"Well, we must prepare. Do you need anything? It is almost time for tea."

"I can wait," Christelle answered timidly.

"It will be our first lesson. We do not have much time."

Lesson? Why did she need lessons? Christelle simply nodded and smiled. Perhaps her ladyship thought her a street urchin.

Armand brought in the tea tray, and Christelle decided she should reassure Lady Ashbury.

"May I pour, *Madame?*"

"*Oui*, I would be delighted."

Christelle tried to maintain a straight face. This had frequently been her task at school. She did not know all of the ways of the English, but Madame Monique had told her it was customary here for the young lady hosting to serve. In Paris, she had served because she was the lowest.

"You do very well, Christelle. Did your school also teach you dancing?"

"*Oui.*"

"And dining?"

"*Oui.*"

Lady Ashbury tapped her nails lightly on the arm of her chair. "How about curtsies?"

"*Oui.*"

"Order of rank?"

"I think it is the same here."

"What of household duties? Accounts? Linens? Menus?"

"*Oui, oui, oui.*" She had to try not to laugh.

"I did not think Harriot's a finishing school," Lady Ashbury murmured with a cocked eyebrow.

Christelle knew these things because she had been required to do them all. Some had even been part of her schooling. She did not wish to confess she had been treated as a servant there.

"Perhaps this will be less difficult than I imagined."

"I hope I will not cause you trouble," Christelle remarked.

"Nonsense. I had thought to teach you things to make you more comfortable amongst the class of people your family associates with—you will not be judged by us."

"I understand why you feel I must need proper training. I was rather desperate when I came to Madame Monique. I am certain there will be things I do not know, but I hope I will not give you cause to blush."

"I do not think so, *chérie*. Monique said you have a few dresses now. Shall we take a look?"

"*Oui*, ones I was able to design. I have not yet purchased slippers and gloves and other such necessities, but Madame said you would be able to help me."

"Of course. This is music to my ears!"

～

"How is that pretty little miss doing? Have you been seeing her often?" Mr. Baker asked as soon as Seamus walked into his office. He was feeling distracted, since he had been reading the note from Christelle over and over on the way there.

"It is nice to see you, Mr. Baker," Seamus remarked with a wry grin.

"Well, the missus said I was to ask, and I did not want to forget," Mr. Baker added.

"Miss Christelle was doing quite well when last I saw her. She is away, visiting her father, as we speak."

"Found him already, did she?"

"It appears that way," he said in a subdued tone. It was hard not to reveal his conflicting emotions.

"She is coming back, ain't she?" Mr. Baker must have heard the sadness in his voice.

"I do not know. I suppose there is a possibility she may not," Seamus answered, realizing, when he said it out loud, he felt a painful void inside.

He became lost in thought for a moment, before he remembered Mr. Baker was there.

"Forgive me. I will be away for a short while to visit my family. My colleague, Dr. Whittier, will be available should you need anything in my absence."

"I will not," Mr. Baker murmured.

"I am pleased with your progress just now. Please give Mrs. Baker my warmest wishes."

"I will. She will expect to see you again for tea, you know."

Seamus smiled. "It will be my pleasure to call on her when I return."

He saw Mr. Baker out, and went home for the day.

He had spent the intervening week in a fit of the dismals, with very little to look forward to. He had received no word from Christelle that she had returned. He had continued to go by the milliner's shop every morning, just in case. He did not expect he would receive any letters from wherever she was. He had no formal claim to her. It was a relief, in a way, to be leaving Town. The hard ride would be welcome to clear his head.

Seamus mounted his black roan, Asclepius, for the journey to Yardley. He longed for Christelle to be there, but he was happy she was finally to meet her father. He wished her well, and he hoped he would be able to find out how she had fared. Selfishly, he wanted to be there with her if she needed comfort. He imagined she would be quite nervous, and if her father was not kind to her... Seamus grew angry even thinking about it. He was hopelessly besotted with Christelle, he had to admit to himself. But Gavin, Margaux, Maili, Iain and Emmaline would all be there and he looked forward to seeing them very much. He did not see them as often as he would like, and it would be a nice respite from his increasingly busy practice.

He passed through the last toll at the city's boundary and let Asclepius have his head. The poor roan had had very little exercise since coming to London. He was a great beast of seventeen hands which Seamus's height required. They would have to stop for the night halfway; it was dark and he preferred to keep his neck intact.

Every stop he made he looked for Christelle. What a pathetically besotted muttonhead he was.

When he rode into Yardley on the evening of his second hard day of riding, he had gone back and forth some hundred times between the happiness he would experience seeing his family and his despair that he might never see Christelle again.

Seamus dismounted and led his horse to the stables. He handed Asclepius over to the groom and asked for his bags to be taken to his room. He was not expected at any particular hour. It was very likely the family was already sitting down for supper. He sneaked in through the back door and up to the nursery. He could not quite wait to see Iain and Emmaline, even covered in all his dirt.

"Seamus!" Iain cried excitedly as he was lifted into the air.

"How is my little brother?"

"I am not a baby any more. I am eight years old, now!" the child insisted when he was on his feet again, looking up at Seamus with his bright blue eyes and black curls.

"Of course you are not a baby. But you will always be my little brother," Seamus said as he ruffled the boy's hair. He took a moment to look around at the nursery, overflowing with children. There were Gavin and Margaux's two, Beaujolais and Yardley's three, and a set of toddler twins he had not yet seen. He suspected those belonged to Anjou and Harris.

"Emmaline? Do you have a hug for your big brother?" he asked the little beauty.

"Say-mus is dirty," she replied with a wrinkled nose.

"I am. A kiss on the cheek, then? I promise to wash immediately."

She leaned over and kissed him lightly on the cheek.

"Is the new girl here yet?" Simone, Yardley's eldest, asked.

"What new girl?"

"*Grandmère* is bringing a young lady. They all suspect 'tis to meet you," she said, proud to know something an adult did not.

Seamus gritted his teeth to keep from groaning. He had not told them of Christelle. He had told Lord Ashbury, but not that he was considering taking her for a wife.

"I must go and change for dinner," he said, while wondering what he was about to walk into.

"Will you come back for bedtime stories?" Emmaline asked.

"Of course!" he answered, feigning offence that she could doubt it.

He went back down to make a proper entrance, wondering who this girl could be who his *grandmère* was bringing to meet him.

CHAPTER 11

*C*hristelle was trembling as they finally pulled through the gates of her father's estate.

"Look. There it is," Lady Ashbury said, pointing to a mansion high up on a hill. It looked grand, even from this distance, and Christelle began to have second thoughts.

For almost two weeks now, she had been staying with Lord and Lady Ashbury, but it still had not eased her mind about meeting her father, the Duke.

The more she heard about him, the more terrified she grew. Lady Ashbury had been trying to acquaint her with his personality, but it had had the opposite effect from the one intended. Her ladyship had spoken of the arguments he and Beaujolais had—all in good humour, of course.

Christelle did not like conflict of any sort. She had hidden when men had yelled at the women on Jersey, and when Lord Dannon or Monsieur Clement had hit her mother, she had wanted to harm them back. The one time she had tried, she had been soundly beaten herself. She had quickly learned when to appear meek.

If her father was like them, she would have to leave. Dr. Craig was nothing like that. He was kind and gentle, and she missed him very much. She would write to him and let him know how it went with her father. She liked to think that he would want to know.

"Christelle? What are you thinking, *chérie?*" Lady Ashbury asked.

"Forgive me. I was wool-gathering."

"You do this quite a bit."

"I was thinking of a friend."

"Ah. *Je comprends.* One you left behind in Paris?" Lady Ashbury asked with a sly glance.

"*Non.* One I met in London."

"It would not do to set your heart on someone yet. Your father will likely expect you to marry as befits the daughter of a Duke."

"He is a gentleman."

"Is he?" Lady Ashbury reached over and patted Christelle's knee. "He will need to be more than any mere gentleman."

"I would hope my father would wish me to be happy."

"Of course. The two need not be exclusive."

"I—" Christelle began to object.

"And remember what we discussed. You are to wait in the parlour until Beaujolais comes to get you. Yardley never ventures in there."

"*Oui,* Madame," Christelle replied wearily. They had been travelling for three days and they had delayed their arrival until this morning. Lord and Lady Ashbury thought it best to approach the Duke in the morning, when he was the least likely to be distracted. To Christelle, that meant when he was least likely to be angry.

At this point, she was ready to have this visit over and done with.

The carriage continued to climb up the hill until the golden stone façade of the house came into view.

"Magnificent, is it not?" Lady Ashbury said whilst watching Christelle's face.

"It is as grand as where the King lives," Christelle answered in awe.

"*Oui.* It is. Your father is a very powerful man in the kingdom."

Christelle sighed. "I wish he was not."

"Why, *mon chérie?*"

"I think he will be less pleased with me."

"He will be more able to provide for you, and see you want for nothing."

"I did not truly want for anything at Madame Monique's."

How could she explain her feelings to this woman who had never known anything but this life? All Christelle wanted was a family— love. She did not bother to make the attempt. The past two weeks had shown her this new family had a different way of life from that to which she was accustomed.

"Here we are, *chérie*. You stay in here until the carriage is taken around to the stables, and a maid will meet you there to take you to the parlour."

"*Oui*, Madame."

Christelle very much disliked playing games. She would have preferred to march to the front door and bang the knocker and introduce herself.

However, the Duke of Yardley did not like surprises, they said, so she did as she was told.

A maid in a starched blue dress was waiting for her in the stable yard. They began to walk towards the back entrance to the house.

Without warning, an enormous black horse came galloping towards them and Christelle could not register what was happening. There was the sound of horseshoes on cobblestone, then sparks flew from iron scraping the stone, voices were shouting warnings...

"*Mon Dieu!*" she exclaimed when she met eyes with the rider. Unable to move, she stood frozen as if watching everything happen as a spectator.

The man jerked on the reins, much to the displeasure of the horse, which skidded and dropped its haunches, unseating the man backwards in an undignified heap onto his posterior.

"Your Grace! I doubt I've seen you unseated since you were in leading strings!" a groom shouted as he came running to his aid. No one seemed to pay him any heed.

"Who are you?" the rider demanded, glowering at Christelle.

He was angry. She had not moved out of his way. She glowered back, then her next instinct was to flee. This was not how she wanted to meet him. Of her parentage, there could be no doubt. She understood why everyone had reacted the way they had in London.

Christelle hiccupped and turned away from the unsettling vision of her own eyes glaring back at her. She put her fist to her mouth and bit down to give an outlet to the pain she felt. Her feet began to carry her behind the stables and across a grassy meadow. She was not quite running, but she could not seem to stop.

She heard voices cry out frantically. "Benedict! Christelle!"

Beaujolais must have realized what was happening when Christelle had not arrived in the parlour, and had come running out to see.

Christelle stopped on a bridge over a river to catch her breath. She put her head down on her arms where they rested on the railing and tried to slow her breathing. What should she do?

She heard footsteps running towards her.

"Please. I want to be alone," she begged as she nervously fingered the pearls around her neck.

She heard the footsteps stop and harsh breathing follow. She could not bear to look up and see the disappointment on his face.

"I cannot allow it."

She threw her head up in astonishment. "I beg your pardon?" she asked defiantly.

He took a step closer, and though her knees were shaking, she stood where she was.

"I do not believe it," he whispered. He reached out and wiped away an errant tear that had escaped down her cheek.

Christelle swallowed hard. Her throat ached from holding back her emotion.

"What is your name, child?"

She opened her mouth to speak, but the words would not come. He was not acting angrily any longer.

"Do not be afraid."

She managed a half smile. "I-I cannot help it."

She looked up into his eyes, which were looking at her with disbelief and perhaps the same wonder she felt. If he had abandoned her, he was a superb actor.

"My name is Christelle, or Christine, which is my given name."

"I am Yardley."

She nodded. Was she to curtsy? This was not how she had rehearsed this first meeting. She looked up at him again and he was opening his arms, and she was pulled into an embrace before she knew what was happening.

"Oh, dear God. I cannot believe I have a daughter I did not know."

He held her tight and she felt him inhale deeply as he placed his face over the top of her head.

She also tried to take in his touch, his scent, the feel—everything about him. He was very tall and he smelled of horses and sandalwood and…he was her father.

He pulled back and looked her over.

"I am astonished. How long have you known about me?"

"Not long. A few weeks perhaps. I did not know if you knew of me, but I had to find you."

He looked off into the distance for several seconds and then moved away from her to lean on the railing.

"I do not know what to think. I had thought your mother no longer had the power to hurt me, but this—"

"I am sorry. I do not wish to interfere with your family."

"No. I did not mean it that way. If I am angry, it is because I have missed almost…seventeen years of your life?" he asked, as if unsure of her exact age.

"*Oui*. I will be seventeen next week."

"How could she keep this from me?" he shouted.

He banged his hand down on the rail and she jumped. He looked at her with sympathy.

"I will never hurt you, child. I am not a violent man, despite what you may hear."

The tender look he gave her told her it was true. It also told her he understood some of what she had seen in her past.

"How did you find me?" he asked as he continued to look her over as she studied him. She did not know if she would ever be able to stop staring. The facial likeness was uncanny, yet he was tall where she was slight; he was imposing where she was ordinary.

"It is quite a story," she began.

"We have the rest of our lives. Start at the beginning," he said with a charming smile, revealing creases around his eyes which told of a better humour than she would have expected after her initial impression of him. She relaxed as he held out his arm for her. "Shall we walk and talk? I can show you the estate, if you wish."

"I would like it very much," she said as she took his arm and allowed him to take her on a tour of the property, still trying to decide if this was real or just another dream.

~

Seamus and Gavin had breakfasted early as was their custom and were enjoying a fireside chat in Yardley's study about Seamus's new practice in London.

"The foxglove seemed miraculous in this patient," Seamus said, explaining Mr. Baker's case. "It was as if his response came straight from the text books."

"So his dropsy and palpitations improved?"

"As long as he takes the prescribed dose, yes. He did double his dose and showed signs of toxicity."

"I am pleased you have found your calling, at last," Gavin said with a proud look.

"I was afraid you would be disappointed," Seamus confessed.

"How could I be disappointed? I have never expected you to love everything I do."

"I very much enjoyed my time at Wyndham. It was rewarding, working with the veterans. I realized I wanted to do more research and become a consulting physician."

"Which is a wise financial decision as well," Gavin pointed out.

"I did not make the decision for money," Seamus said. "I confess I was motivated by something else."

Gavin wrinkled his brow, as if trying to determine what Seamus was referring to.

"I want a family."

"A family? Then I would have expected to see you return to Scotland."

"You misunderstand me. I would like a family of my own. There was only a small selection in Sussex."

"Ah." Gavin gave a smile laced with understanding. "So you went to London for a certain female?"

Seamus chuckled. "I had no one in mind when I left, but it does appear as though fate knew what it was doing."

"Shall I bring Margaux in to hear the story? I will never re-tell it properly."

"If you wish."

Gavin went to the nearby breakfast room, where the three sisters, Margaux, Beaujolais and Anjou, were eating, returning shortly with Margaux. Seamus stood to kiss his step-mother. "Good morning."

"Good morning. *Maman* and *Papa* arrived a few minutes ago. She was telling us about her guest." She sat on the arm of Gavin's chair. "Now Gavin says you have a story to share? Pray tell!"

"I was about to regale him with how I met a young lady by coincidence... or accident, I suppose."

Margaux smiled. "Oh, Seamus!" She clasped her hands together.

"I do hope *Grandmère* will not be too disappointed. Simone said she was bringing a young lady to meet me."

"Nonsense. She is never disappointed. I think the visitor is intended to meet Yardley, anyway."

"Oh? Capital!" he said with relief. "Well, I was walking across the bridge towards Westminster, when I ran into someone on the pavement."

"Oh, dear. Are they all right?" she asked.

"Yes, quite well. More than *quite* well. It turned out to be a lady. She had just arrived from Paris and could not find her way." Seamus omitted the unnecessary details.

Gavin and Margaux exchanged glances.

"I helped her find her way, and I have been seeing her once a week since then."

"Did she come alone?" Margaux asked with concern.

"Yes. It is a sad story. She was orphaned, or at least she thought she was, until she found her birth certificate. So, she came to England to find her father. *Grandpère* gave her a reference and thus Madame Monique employed her as a seamstress."

"Oh, no!" Margaux said, covering her mouth.

Had he said something wrong? He had thought his parents would be delighted.

Just then, they heard a commotion from behind the house. A horse was neighing; there was a screech of metal on stone, and there was general mêlée.

Someone was shouting 'Benedict' and he thought he heard 'Christelle.'

"Christelle?" Seamus repeated aloud. Was it possible there was a coincidence? Margaux and Gavin had already run out to the terrace to see what the commotion was. Perhaps he should see if someone was hurt.

He followed the crowd and caught a glimpse of a petite blonde, hurrying away across the meadow. Yardley was dusting himself off and looking over to his wife.

"It was not supposed to happen like this," she said, her head in her hands, weeping. "I wanted to tell you about her first."

"I will go to her," Yardley said and he set off across the meadow after the girl.

The whole group of them, family, grooms, the coachman and two footmen, stood there and watched him run until both Yardley and the girl were out of sight.

"What has happened?" Seamus asked, though deep down inside he knew.

"Yardley had a daughter by Lillian who he did not know about. She recently arrived from France and has been working as a seamstress in London," Margaux explained, almost reciting what he himself had just described a few moments before.

Seamus closed his eyes in self-reprimanding disbelief. "How could I have not seen it?"

Margaux put her hand on his arm and gave him a look of sympathy.

Should this not be good news? He had been concerned whether his family would accept a modiste, and now he would not be considered worthy enough?

"I need a drink," Lord Ashbury stated to no one in particular.

"It was not supposed to happen this way," Beaujolais kept repeating as her mother and sisters led her away.

Gavin patted him on the shoulder and left him alone.

As the family returned to the house, and the servants went back to work, Seamus could only stand there, feeling as though his world had been turned inside out.

Why was he thinking only of himself? What of Christelle? How would she feel now? Would she be different? Very likely she had not even thought of him since leaving London, what with meeting her father—and what a father, to be sure.

Seamus needed to step back and give them time. His heart gave a painful squeeze inside his chest. Clearly, it did not agree. He had lived long enough to know Christelle was the person he wanted to spend his life with—to have a family with. However, she had just found her father after a lifetime without one, and a mother who should remain nameless. Seamus had never met her, but had heard tell of her antics and how they had almost caused Beaujolais and Yardley to be killed instead of her.

Abruptly, Seamus noticed he was freezing, which was not surprising, since he had neglected to put on his coat before coming outdoors and it was only February. He walked back into the house, wondering if it would be best for him to return to London.

CHAPTER 12

*C*hristelle and Yardley walked to the edge of the still and serene lake before he spoke. "How does one go about catching up on seventeen years?"

"I do not think it is possible," she replied softly.

"Perhaps not. My first inclination is to have you try to recite every detail. Where did you live? What is your favourite colour? Your favourite food? Your favourite pastimes? Who has taken care of you all these years since Lil...since your *maman* died?"

"I do not think I want to remember it all," she said, wrinkling her nose.

"What would you like me to know about you, then?" he asked with a look of amusement.

"Let me think. I love pastel colours—all of them. They make me think of flowers in spring. I love the smell of the garden after the rain."

He closed his eyes and smiled. "It will not be long now until the estate is covered in blooms. I hope you will enjoy them."

"My favourite food is anything sweet. I was not allowed desserts at school these past six years," she said with a sideways glance.

"The cheese-paring wretches! I do think we can remedy that." He was making an effort to be light-hearted, at least. They walked a few steps down the path and he looked down at her. "You have been at a school? In Paris?"

"Yes. As a charity pupil. *Maman* left me there before coming to England."

"I see. Were you happy there?" he asked. His voice sounded thick with emotion, whether because of sadness or some other thing she could not tell.

She slightly lifted one shoulder. "I was content. It was better than the alternative."

He swallowed hard. She wished she knew what he was thinking. He had taken the news better than she had imagined, after all the others had said of him.

She watched his face as discreetly as she could. She wanted to memorize every angle, every line. It appeared as though he was struggling between anger and disbelief when he was looking away, but by the time he looked at her, he had composed his features again.

"Are you cold? I confess I have been so astonished I have taken leave of courtesy."

"No, I am quite content. I am enjoying viewing the park."

"Then we shall continue to the hidden treasure, if you like," he said, with the smile of a school-boy.

"Lead the way," she responded, smiling in return.

"Where did you live before you went to school?" He continued to ask questions.

Maybe one day she would be brave enough to ask all she wished.

"Mostly on Jersey. Do you know of it? It is an island in the Channel," she replied.

He stopped and swung around. His face held an expression of disbelief.

She met his gaze. "Yes. I lived on Jersey—on Lord Dannon's estate. My *maman* was a high-paid courtesan."

"You knew all of this?" He searched her face. The pain in his eyes was evident.

"She did try to keep me away from there once she realized I understood. But it was better than being in Paris with Monsieur Clement."

He made another noise that sounded distinctly like a growl. He then looked to the sky and took a deep breath. It was obvious he was having difficulty keeping his temper in check by the way he clenched his jaw.

"Why did you not care for Monsieur Clement?"

Christelle hesitated, and her father noticed.

"Did he hurt you?"

"Only if I interfered with *Maman's* business. I learned very young to stay out of his sight."

"And Dannon?"

"The situation was much the same. *Maman* did try to keep me away from him. She said he preferred girls my age, so she sent me to school instead of bringing me to England with her."

"It is a good thing they are dead," he said. His voice was frighteningly calm.

He walked on and was silent for a while as they traversed a pathway upwards from the lake and along the river. She could see his temple pulsing and he was clenching his fists. She would happily avoid telling him these things, but he wanted to know. They came to a canopy of greenery that seemed to be woven through trees, and he stepped behind an opening in a hedge she would have not noticed on her own. She followed him through and saw a beautiful waterfall flowing down the side of the hill.

Christelle gasped with appreciation. She had never seen one before. Both she and her father watched as the water seemed to trickle in some places and beat hard against the rocks in others. It made a rushing sound and left a mist behind in the cool air before flowing away into the river. She could have watched it for hours.

"The water is much stronger in the spring after the snow and ice has melted. But you will enjoy watching it in all seasons. But, come, let us return to the house. They will be wondering where we have gone to for so long. Your nose is red, and I am beginning to become chilled myself."

"I confess, I am cold too, but I do not wish to leave."

"I always feel the same. It will be here for you whenever you wish to view it."

He led her back down the path with a guiding hand, though her footing was sure in her boots, and took her arm and brought her close. The warmth was welcome as they came back out into the meadow and out of the protection of the trees. Her wool dress and pelisse were beginning to feel thin.

"How did you come to be here now, Christelle?"

"The school asked me to leave and I could not find a position in Paris. I had found my certificate of birth in my *maman's* effects, so I decided to come here to look for you. A very nice gentleman helped me find employment at Madame Monique's in London. She recognized me and sent me to Lady Ashbury."

"A nice, *honourable* gentleman?" His voice wavered.

"Yes, very honourable. He is a physician, and said he has two sisters near to my age."

"Thank God. Do you know what could have happened to you?"

"I am well aware," she said softly. "Unfortunately, your wife saw me in the shop and received quite a shock, though she was also very kind. I cannot imagine what she must feel."

"Yes, I am surprised she did not tell me sooner." He looked away.

"She had intended to tell you before you saw me. That was the plan. She did not wish for you to meet me on the street in London as she did." Christelle felt the need to defend her.

"I see."

He appeared to ponder this. Was he angry with Lady Beaujolais for not telling him sooner?

"Give her time, she will come to care for you," he added, but he looked irritated. "It is a blessing you do not resemble Lillian."

"I do not intend to be trouble for your wife or you. I am thankful I have had a chance to meet you."

"Do not speak as though I will not see you again," he chided.

"I would like that very much. But I do have a good home and I enjoy my work."

"Enough!" he said sternly. "Your home is with me. I am not going to let you leave the moment I have found you."

"Thank you, sir," she said, surprised—and warmed—by his vehemence.

"Papa," he corrected.

"Papa," she repeated slowly, trying the words on her tongue for the first time. "I never thought to say that."

"Oh, child." He took her into his arms. "You have me now. We have each other now. What would you care to do next? Or do you need to rest? We need not hurry."

"May I meet my siblings? I have always wanted brothers and sisters."

"You have come to the right family. Jolie and I have three together, and her sisters have several offspring as well. Margaux's step-children are nearer your age, and two of them are here now. Catriona married some years ago."

"A large family sounds a dream come true. I think I would like to start with my own siblings first."

"Very well, to the nursery we go." He began to stride with purpose.

"Will they mind?" she asked, having second thoughts.

"Fortunately, I think they are too young to be anything but delighted."

She let out a laugh that could have been mistaken for a giggle. It was hard not to run to the house with anticipation. This meeting had exceeded her expectations.

"One more thing...Papa?"

"Anything."

"Can you teach me about horses? Unfortunately, I was not permitted to ride at school."

"I would be delighted. Your mother was an excellent horsewoman, you know."

"I remember riding a pony with her when I was small."

She could feel his arm tense under his coat.

"It will return to you quickly."

"I do think I would prefer to learn a less dramatic dismount," she suggested dryly.

"You minx!" he answered with an appreciative laugh.

∼

Seamus retired to the nursery to spend more time with the children. He was not prepared to face the adults and all their questions about Christelle. He had all but confessed his feelings for her to Gavin and Margaux. He never could have foreseen such an unlikely coincidence!

"Seamus!" The children cried his name when he appeared in the nursery. All of them jumped to their feet and ran to mob him.

He looked guiltily towards the nurses and mouthed, "My apologies."

He was not sure why he loved children so much. Perhaps it was from his time in the orphanage. It had been necessary to help with the younger ones there. He had discovered early on that it was easier to play with them than to scold them.

"Say-mus?" Little Emmaline tugged his sleeve. "May we play Rescue the Damsel?"

"May the children have some playtime now?" he asked one of the three nurses standing nearby.

The nurses were smiling, so they could not be too angry. One of them nodded and said, "I think it would be acceptable."

"I will be the princess who has been kidnapped in the tower," Simone pronounced.

"Why do you always get to be the princess?" Emmaline asked, putting her hands on her hips.

"Because I am the oldest girl," Simone stated.

Seamus had to hide a smile.

"And you can be the knight in shining armour who rides gallantly on his steed to rescue me," Simone said to Iain.

"What shall we be?" the other children asked.

"Emmy, you may be his squire. Rosie, you can be my handmaiden, and Francis, you can be the evil villain."

"What about me?" Seamus asked.

"The horsey!" all of the children replied in unison. He was always the horsey.

Seamus chuckled and began to remove his coat and waistcoat. He rolled up his sleeves and removed his boots. Nursery games were no place for dignity, especially when he was to be the horse. "What is my name to be?" he asked as he got down on all fours and into position.

"Copenhagen," Iain announced.

"An excellent choice," he agreed as his brother mounted his back and the other children took their places.

"Tally ho!" Iain commanded as Simone began to wail, 'Save me! Save me!' from her position atop the table.

Seamus commenced making trotting noises and moved forward as Francis jumped in front of him with his wooden sword.

Iain dismounted and a fencing match ensued to the cheers of all of the other children. Once Seamus had to intervene when Francis became too intent on killing his rival.

Iain gained the upper hand and Francis died admirably, thumping on to the floor with a loud groan and limbs splayed convincingly.

Iain eventually managed to rescue Simone and both of them were safely on his back and galloping away when the Duke appeared in the doorway of the nursery.

"Papa!" Rosie shouted and took off towards Yardley.

The nursemaids immediately began rounding up their charges, while Seamus remained on all fours with his head down, chastising himself. How could he not have realized who Christelle was? Rosalind and Christelle looked just like Yardley. Standing up, he had begun to brush off his knees and pull down his shirtsleeves when he noticed Christelle was standing there staring at him.

"Dr. Craig! What are you doing here?"

"Lady Christelle." He bowed before running his hand through his hair to smooth it, as if he had any shred of dignity left.

"You two know each other?" the Duke asked, looking back and forth between the two of them.

Christelle smiled. "Yes, this is the gentleman who rescued me."

"Seamus?"

"It is true, sir, though I did not realize who she was until a few moments ago. I cannot believe I did not see it before."

"It is rather an uncanny resemblance. Do not berate yourself, Women tend to be more adept at these things. I am grateful you were there to help her," Yardley answered. His tone was sincere.

Seamus inclined his head. There was little else to say without the Duke making wrong assumptions.

"Papa, who is your guest?" Simone asked with all of her dignity, as though she had not just been screaming indignantly from her princess's tower.

"Ah, yes. Lady Christelle, may I introduce to you your sisters and brother: Lady Simone, Lord Stanton and Lady Rosalind."

"A sister?" Simone asked as she cocked her head to the side.

"It is astonishing, is it not? You know I told you I was married before."

Simone nodded.

"I found out today that I had a daughter I did not know about."

Simone looked more closely at Christelle before smiling. She stepped forward and curtsied deeply before her. "I am pleased to make your acquaintance, sister."

"And I yours." Christelle returned the curtsy and came up with tears of joy in her eyes. Francis and Rosalind also greeted her, but with a bit more exuberance.

"Is Rosalind a family name? It was also one of my given names," Christelle asked Yardley.

"It is my mother's name," Yardley answered, still looking as if he was struggling to contain his emotions.

"You will not get to be the princess in the tower now," Rosalind said to Simone.

"Oh, no," Christelle said as she shook her head. "I have already been rescued." She looked over to Seamus with a smile which melted his heart. He wished no one else was there to watch.

"I must take Christelle to meet the rest of the family," Yardley said.

"So soon?"

"Perhaps she can return after tea to spend more time with you all and meet the rest of the children."

"I would like that very much," Christelle assured the children.

"Seamus, will you join us?" Yardley asked with a penetrating look.

Seamus had stepped back from the scene in order to don his coat and attempt to repair his neck-cloth, which had been used for reins. He had been very much caught off-guard by Yardley's invitation and would have preferred to remain invisible for the moment.

"I am certain everyone will wish to hear of how you found and rescued Christelle," the Duke was saying.

Seamus looked around at all the faces staring at him in awe. He would very much prefer to stay here and play horsey than face the Ashbury inquisition. However, he could not politely refuse.

"Of course, I would be delighted," he said instead.

CHAPTER 13

There were so many people in the room, and it would be very difficult to keep them all organized in her head. Christelle looked around the parlour, which was elegant yet simple. It was similar in size to the Ashbury drawing room in London, but felt much smaller with the entire family in occupation. The walls were covered in heavily gilded frames of stern-looking ancestors, she presumed, interspersed with some landscapes. The draperies and the carpets were of red tones and the walls and ceiling were ivory. The room was flanked with matching fireplaces, and there were several sofas arranged for conversing.

There were three Beaujolais! Then she recognized Lord and Lady Ashbury, of course, and it seemed there was a husband for each of the triplet sisters. Seamus walked over to a girl who appeared to be near her own age and shared the same colouring as Dr. Craig. She must be one of his sisters.

It would be very difficult to remain calm and not become overwhelmed. Everyone had risen to their feet and all of their faces were staring at her.

"I expect you have all heard that this is my daughter, Christelle." Her father pointed towards where Seamus Craig stood near a family.

"Let me introduce you to everyone you have not met. This is Lord Craig and his wife, Margaux, Lady Craig. As you can no doubt surmise, they are Dr. Craig's parents, and this is his sister, Maili."

"We are very pleased to make your acquaintance, Lady Christelle," Lord Craig said. He had kind eyes and a gentle manner much like his son. Lady Craig smiled at her very kindly.

"And this is Lord Harris and his wife, Anjou, Lady Harris. Margaux and Anjou are the sisters of Beaujolais."

"Yes, I can see the resemblance." Christelle smiled.

"Welcome to the family." Anjou added her voice to the greetings. Her husband was handsome, though he looked like a pirate.

"Please take a seat and we can ring for tea." Beaujolais gestured towards a sofa with scrolled armrests. Christelle noticed that her father had joined his wife and had taken her hand, discreetly smoothing his thumb back and forth over it.

Christelle hoped she was not causing too much distress between them. She would very much like some time alone now, to try to think through everything that had happened, but she sat down and tried to make herself pleasing. Dr. Craig came to sit in the chair nearby and she relaxed.

"This is quite a surprise," he said quietly.

"Yes, but I am grateful for a familiar face."

"That is good to hear," he commented. "I still cannot believe I did not realize who you were from the beginning."

"*Non.* Why would you have? We only see the things we expect to see."

"Are you rubbing along well with Yardley?"

"I believe so. He has been very kind and accepted the news better than I could have hoped."

"I am relieved to hear it. You look very tired. I imagine this has been quite an ordeal."

"I am not used to so much attention and my nerves were quite on edge beforehand," she admitted.

"I think it would be understandable if you asked to rest. No one would think the worse of you."

"I want to, but equally I do not want to. I know it does not make sense."

"If you need time for quiet reflection, just ask." He leaned in close and she could smell his comforting musky scent.

"I think a walk later would be very welcome."

"Christelle, pray tell us how you and Seamus came to know one another?" Beaujolais asked, interrupting their private cose.

She could feel heat rising to colour her face. She was not prepared for answering these questions in front of the entire family.

"Christelle and I happened upon each other by accident," Seamus said, filling in the uncomfortable silence. "She had just arrived from Paris and was not certain in which direction to go, so I helped her. *Grandpère* was kind enough to tell us which modiste the family used, and I took her to Madame Monique. She recognized Lady Christelle, whereas I did not."

"What an uncanny coincidence. It has all turned out well, though, has it not?" Lord Ashbury asked.

"Will you be coming out this Season?" Maili asked.

Christelle had no idea what she meant. Her face must have showed her confusion.

"She means *dèbut*," Margaux explained. "Maili is of age and will be going to London for what we call the Season."

"It is balls and parties and rides in the park," Maili said wistfully. "It would be great fun to share it with my new cousin."

Christelle looked over to Yardley, who was watching her intently.

"I think sharing the Season would be an excellent idea, if Christelle is comfortable with it," Lady Ashbury agreed.

"We have plenty of time to make those decisions," Yardley said.

Childers and another servant brought in the tea tray and a tray of delicacies.

The focus was taken from Christelle as the family served tea and carried on conversations between themselves. Her father and Beaujolais were in an intimate conversation, while Maili joined her and Seamus.

Maili was bright and cheerful. She had a pleasant, unassuming manner and seemed well pleased with everyone and everything. Christelle felt envious of her open, easy ways, but also felt comfortable with her. She had the same auburn hair and grey eyes of her brother, but appeared more radiant, most likely because of her personality.

"Are you eighteen?" Maili asked boldly.

"I will be seventeen on this day next week," Christelle answered, keeping her eyes on her tea-cup. She did not wish to look Dr. Craig in the eye. Would he think her too juvenile?

"Splendid!" Maili exclaimed. "We have an excuse for a party."

"No, I do not think..." Christelle started to object.

"Maili, can you not see Christelle is quite overwhelmed already?" Seamus chided gently.

"Oh." Maili cocked her head and appeared to consider it.

"Let us allow her to become acclimatized to her new circumstances before we arrange her social calendar for the next twelvemonth."

"I beg your pardon, Lady Christelle," Maili said, pouting prettily. "I am so delighted to have a cousin of my own age, I forgot my manners."

"There is nothing to forgive," Christelle said. "I, too, am very happy to have a family."

Maili cast a contemptuous glance at Seamus, though Christelle saw it. Maili excused herself to go and speak to Margaux.

"Maili does not remember what it was like before. She was very young when our parents died. She has never seemed to be as affected as Catriona and I were," he explained, setting his tea-cup down in its saucer on the table.

"I would say that is a blessing."

"Yes, I suppose it is. But when she seems younger than you, although she is almost a year older, you may understand why."

Christelle could feel heat rising within her. He appreciated her maturity, and it gave her pleasure. Part of her wished she could leave with Dr. Craig at this very moment.

"Do not let them force you into anything with which you are not comfortable. The Ashbury family is quite a force in the *ton* and do not always understand everyone does not wish for notoriety."

"I think if you will be near, most anything will be acceptable to me."

Seamus let out a deep sigh.

"What is the matter?" she asked with concern. Something was bothering him.

He hesitated to answer. "Nothing. Nothing is the matter. I will always be here for you." He looked up at her and smiled, though she could see doubt in his eyes.

～

The next morning, Seamus thought to catch Christelle early before she was monopolized again—and invite her for a walk. Yesterday, after tea, she had delighted in playing with the children, then following dinner, there had been a friendly Ashbury game of charades. Friendly also meant competitive to a fault. There had been a few moments in which to speak to Christelle, but there was always someone else within earshot.

He did love his family—every idiosyncratic bit—but they would be shocked at the number of times he had contemplated throwing Christelle over his shoulder and running from the room. It would have taken everyone else a while to realize it was not part of the game. He laughed. He should have done it. It had looked as though it would be his best hope to have time alone with her.

The breakfast room was still empty by the time he finished his meal and second cup of coffee. It had been a late night, but his body was unaccustomed to sleeping past six, no matter how tired he was.

He walked into the entry hall and there was still no sign of life in the household. He decided to go for a walk and take in some fresh air.

When he passed by the study, with its doors still closed, he overheard voices.

"Perhaps Maili is right. We should take her to Town for the Season."

"I am not certain she will enjoy it."

Seamus did not want to overhear the intimate conversation between Yardley and Beaujolais. He put on his great coat and hat as quickly as possible but still was privy to more than he wished.

"What will everyone say when they see her?"

"At least she does not look like Lillian?" Yardley replied mockingly.

"Thank God for that, but no. Someone is bound to tell her how her mother died. Perhaps it would be best to tell her now."

"I think it would be too much. It will not be easy, either way. Let her get to know you first."

"I do not like having secrets between us. It will be hard enough for her to accept me."

"I do not agree. She is nothing like Lillian. She is eager to please."

"She appears to be," Beaujolais agreed.

"And when she knows you as I do..." Yardley's voice lowered and trailed off.

There was a moment of silence and Seamus wished he was both invisible and deaf, but the front door was locked.

"I take it back. I do not want her to know you in quite the same fashion," Yardley went on in a seductive tone.

"Benedict, this is serious."

"We survived the problem of Lillian, we will survive this," he said, his tone serious again. "I am a duke, you are a duchess. She is our daughter, and if we accept her as such, so will the rest of the world."

"What if she wishes to remain plain Miss Christelle Stanton, modiste?"

"There is nothing plain about her. If she wished to remain anonymous, she should not have come."

"I do not think that is quite fair."

"Perhaps I am being severe. I will not be overbearing, but I do want her to have every opportunity she is entitled to as our daughter."

Seamus tried to move away but the floor creaked and he froze. Could he not be honourable and leave the eavesdropping without appearing guilty?

"What would you hope for her?" Beaujolais asked Yardley.

"A happy home, a place in our family, a rightful place in Society, and a suitable marriage, to begin with," he rattled off.

"It seems so sudden."

"A bit of a fairytale, yes. But with you to bring her out, I have no doubt she will have her prince and a happy ending."

"If that is your wish... and hers."

There was deafening silence yet again, and Seamus decided to make a run for it. No doubt the servants knew which floorboards creaked, but he did not wish to hear or imagine any more. He dashed through the house down the stairs to the kitchen with a greeting and a smile and inhaled deeply of the crisp winter air when he had reached the safety of the outdoors.

Seamus walked down the path from the house, drawn to the serenity of the glassy water. He stood on the stone bridge for some time watching waterfowl soar and swoop down from the round temple guarding the lake. He knew he must allow Christelle to have this Season without interference from him, reflecting about what was on his conscience. She did seem to return his regard, but that might change when other more attractive suitors and titles pursued her in earnest. And Yardley might not approve of his suit. Either way, she needed time before he courted her. It would be difficult to stand back and watch, but he knew it was right.

He felt more at ease by the time he began his return trip. As he was coming up the path, Yardley was walking out towards him.

"Good morning, Seamus."

"Good morning, sir." Seamus was still uncomfortable calling him Yardley, even though he had been his uncle for well over a decade. Yardley fell in step with him and they walked side-by-side back to the house.

"The men are shooting to fill the larder. Will you join us?"

Seamus hesitated.

"The ladies are going into the village this morning, and if the weather holds, they have a pall-mall re-match planned for the afternoon. Heaven help us all."

"Yes, of course. I am a bit rusty with a fowling piece," Seamus confessed.

"Fret not. Harris will get your share and then some."

Seamus was quite a good shot, but he never had liked killing things. It went against his nature as a physician.

"I did want to repeat my gratefulness to you—in earnest, for saving Christelle. I know you are a good man—and when I think of what could have happened..." Yardley's voice cracked.

"Yes. It was not a stretch for my imagination, either. It could have easily been one of my sisters." Would he be so thankful if he knew how he truly felt about her?

Yardley looked away for a few steps, then stopped. "Seamus, I would like to do something for you."

Seamus could not think of what he meant. "Thanking me is enough."

"I would like to show you my gratitude."

"Just for helping a lost girl from a bridge who would have frozen to death? I could not accept it, sir. It would not be right. I had no idea she was your daughter, and I would have helped her, regardless."

Yardley stared at him, and though uncomfortable, Seamus held his gaze. Yardley was not used to being told no, but this was a matter of integrity.

"I beg your pardon," Yardley said softly. "I intended no offence."

Seamus inclined his head.

"However, I feel I should do something!" he persisted.

"Sir," Seamus began.

"Benedict or Yardley, please. Even Uncle is preferable to sir!"

"Very well, Yardley. Nevertheless, seeing Lady Christelle welcomed here has been thanks enough. I confess I will miss spending Wednesday afternoons with her, but she deserves this."

"What precisely were you doing on Wednesdays?" Yardley looked sideways at him.

"I took her to Astley's; walking in the park, once..."

"This is a dilemma."

"How so? It was all very proper, sir."

"But she had no chaperone, and you must have been seen. Although you are cousins..."

Seamus thought back to Lord and Lady Roth, and knew what he said was likely true. He would dearly love to ask for her hand in marriage at that very moment, but he could sense Yardley was not ready to part with his daughter yet. They needed time together. And would he consider an adopted physician to be good enough for her?

CHAPTER 14

*T*he ladies are going into the village this morning," Maili informed Christelle as she walked in from the adjoining room. The two of them were sharing a sitting room, and Christelle had been indulging in reading a book—something she rarely ever had chance to do. Reluctantly, she tore her eyes away from the page.

What was she expected to say? *Have a pleasant outing?*

"Well, are you not coming with us?" Maili looked confused.

"Oh. I did not know I was supposed to."

Maili's mouth twisted a little to the side. "Perhaps I should have asked you rather than told you. I assumed you would know you were invited."

"I was never invited on such excursions while at school. I did not understand what you meant."

"I never went to school," Maili confessed as she twirled a curl which hung over her shoulder. "I suppose there were lessons at the orphanage and we had a governess at the castle."

"A castle?"

"Yes." Maili laughed. "This is just as grand, though I don't believe it has a dungeon."

"I am afraid to know where the other sister lives," Christelle muttered.

"Oh, they have an ordinary house, but they do sometimes live on their boat."

Christelle knew her eyes must be wide with curiosity. What an extraordinary family she had come into. "What shall we do in the village?" Christelle asked.

"Buy ribbons and gloves, visit with the villagers, that sort of thing. Mama says it is our duty to support the tenants and such. The men are going shooting, which sounds more fun to me."

"Do you like to hunt?" Christelle had never thought of ladies hunting.

"Certainly!" Maili exclaimed. "John taught me. He is married to my sister, Catriona. You will have to visit Scotland to meet them. He was injured in the war and does not travel often."

Christelle stood and placed her book on the stand. "I will need a bonnet and pelisse, I think."

"Some boots would be useful also," Maili replied following her into her room. "What are these?" she asked, noticing some of Christelle's sketches on the desk.

"A hobby now, I suppose," she said wistfully as she tied the ribbons on her bonnet.

"These are glorious!" Maili glanced back and forth between Christelle and one of the sketches. "Why, this is the one you are wearing!"

Christelle smiled. "It is. Madame helped me to make it before I left."

"I forgot you were working for Madame Monique. I hope to have new gowns soon. I've always wanted to dance at real balls and drive in the park. Oh, and go to the theatre!" She leaned against the dressing table and threw her hand to her forehead in dramatic illustration. "*Oh Romeo, Romeo! Wherefore art thou, Romeo?* I have always enjoyed theatricals. I wonder if we might put a play on before we leave?"

"Should we not be meeting the others?" Christelle asked, hoping to divert Maili from this line of thought. She could think of no horror greater than performing on the stage with thousands of eyes upon her.

"Oh, yes! I had already forgotten!"

Christelle followed her out of the room, wondering what it would be like to feel so carefree? To worry about nothing other than parties and handsome men? Perhaps that was a bit unfair. She did not know Maili well yet.

All four of the ladies were waiting for them in the entry hall.

"What a lovely gown, Christelle," Beaujolais remarked.

"It is one of her own designs," Maili proclaimed.

"Is it? I believe I had best consult you in the future," Anjou said to Christelle.

"It would be wise to keep it our little secret," Lady Ashbury said. "With so many of us to accoutre, she will run out of ideas."

And they did not wish anyone to know, Christelle knew. She had no intention of stopping what she enjoyed, even if it was only for family.

They took two carriages, one with the ducal crest, and the other with that of the Marquessate. They were not travelling incognito, to say the least. Christelle sat forward facing, next to Lady Ashbury.

"I think the best approach is to answer questions honestly but succinctly," the Lady announced. "It is best to present her to everyone before the outcry has a chance to start."

"Do you mean me?"

"Of course, *chérie*. We are taking this excursion to show you off in the village."

Christelle had to bite her inner lip to keep her face impassive—a trick she had learned long ago at Harriot's. She felt a sudden longing for Dr. Craig. They should be walking and talking now. Instead, she was to be paraded around and forced to meet strangers.

"You will become accustomed, my dear. But for a little while you will be very much on display, and people will be curious."

"It is a fantastic thing," Beaujolais said quietly. "I still cannot believe, though I see you with my own eyes."

113

"I understand. It is how I feel when I see my father. To think all of these years he never knew of my existence."

"Did you enjoy meeting the children?" Beaujolais asked kindly.

"Very much so. Rosalind and I favour each other. In temperament and looks."

"It is how I knew you immediately," Beaujolais confessed.

"I think Maili's temperament is more suited to this Season you speak of. I do not enjoy large gatherings—or being the centre of attention."

"It is a necessity, *chérie*. Margaux did not enjoy it either, but you will be a success. No doubt suitors will be lining the streets for your hand," put in Lady Ashbury.

Christelle looked at Beaujolais for help. She seemed to give her a sympathetic look.

"Here we are!" Lady Ashbury pronounced. "Let us see if we can find some more accessories to complete your trousseau."

"More? But we purchased enough in London to last for years."

Lady Ashbury simply laughed as they alighted.

Beaujolais leaned over and whispered, "Just nod and smile. It is futile to protest."

Why did Christelle feel her wishes were becoming more and more disregarded with each passing day?

How long should she allow this to continue? It seemed as though she was losing control of herself, though everyone appeared to have her best interests at heart. It did not mean it was what she wanted.

How many more fowl must die before they would be done? Seamus wondered as the gunpowder smoke wafted around him. It felt as though they had been shooting for hours. He had felled two birds, which was enough for both him and Christelle's portions, but the other men had continued to shoot and the spaniels to retrieve their kills.

"I suppose we should return soon. I know the ladies were wishing to play games this afternoon," Yardley remarked in a half-hearted manner to no one in particular.

Harris and Gavin groaned aloud.

"Yes, I know, but we must humour them from time to time," he added sympathetically. "The trick is to play like they are men. Do not treat them as ladies."

"I would not dare!" Harris said with scorn. "I enjoy every minute of watching them lose."

Seamus and Gavin laughed. The sisters did not care for losing.

"I do not enjoy sleeping in the other room, however," Gavin added.

"Victory is bitter-sweet, eh?" Harris asked with a knowing glance.

"Very much so."

The men handed their rifles to the accompanying servants and began the mile trek back to the house. They watched the carriages coming up the drive conveying the ladies, and greeted them at the door before they went in to wash and change their raiment.

"How did you fare in the village?" Yardley asked as he helped Christelle and Beaujolais down.

Beaujolais let out a deep sigh. "We ran into the rector and his wife."

"It was bound to happen soon, if not today," he remarked.

"Yes, but now the entire village will know before tea."

"It was what we wanted. We will carry on as normal. Anyone who does not approve may move to another village."

Seamus listened with admiration. What must it be like to be a duke?

"Are we still in order for our match today?" Yardley was asking.

"I think I would prefer a rest after tea," Beaujolais answered.

Yardley wrinkled his brow. "Are you unwell?"

Seamus's ears perked up at the familiar word.

"No. Just fagged."

Seamus was relieved. He would much rather escort Christelle on a walk at the moment than either play a game or attend the Duchess.

Christelle was still surrounded by the other ladies and he feared he would never have a moment with her again. But they began to retire upstairs with their husbands and he caught her glance. He was conscious of his shooting attire and dirty boots, but he was afraid to miss the small chance. He manoeuvred his way to her side.

"Have you enjoyed your excursion?"

"Everyone has been very kind," she said with a tired-looking smile that said more than her words.

"Would you care to take a walk later? At least around the gardens?" he asked hopefully.

"May we go now?" She surprised him by asking.

"If you do not mind me as I am."

"*Non.* I have seen many sides of you on this trip," she said with an amused twinkle in her eye.

"I hope they do not offend."

"On the contrary. They are all equally charming."

He led her around the side of the house to the landscaped garden. It was more wild and natural, in the Capability Brown style, than the manicured parterre gardens set out at the front of the imposing mansion.

When they were finally alone and some distance from the house, she asked, "Are they always this *passionate?*"

"Who? The family? I am afraid so. When they are all together it is quite..." He paused, searching for the right word.

"Overwhelming," she answered, sitting down on a nearby bench.

"You must tell them. They can certainly *come it too strong*, if you will forgive the expression. Lady Ashbury likes everything to be extravagant and grandiose."

"I had noticed. I could not dissuade her from buying another bonnet and two more pairs of gloves today, though she had purchased me over a dozen in London. On the other hand, however, I do not wish to offend my new family."

"That is understandable."

"What is this Season they and your sister speak of?"

"It is, somewhat unkindly, known as the Marriage Mart—amongst bachelors anyway."

"So, I am to be taken there and somebody will choose me as a wife." It was not a question.

"It is wrapped up in a prettier package than that, but essentially, yes. There will be dinners and balls and parties, as well as the theatre and rides in the park; it is a few weeks of madcap courting."

"It sounds horrid."

"Many people live for the Season. Maili has been dreaming of it since she knew what it was."

"But she has been raised for it. I have not."

"You must not feel as if you are being forced into anything. Do not allow it. Your family wants you to have the best of everything and this is their way of showing it." If she only knew how he ached inside to have to say these things when he longed to have her for his own.

"Extravagance. What an interesting perspective. I confess, I had not thought of it in such a way, but perhaps you are correct. I will try to remember it. Will you be part of this Season?"

"I will attend a few things. Of course, I will put in an appearance at anything our family hosts, which I expect to be often this Season with you and Maili there."

"Are there truly several events every single night?"

"Yes, truly."

She sighed and he could hear the resignation in her voice.

"Will you promise me one thing?"

"Of course," she said looking up at him with innocent eyes.

"Send word to me if you need anything."

"But how?"

"Leave a note with Childers. He will make sure I receive it."

"Childers? The butler?"

"I took care of him while he was recuperating after the war. He will be discreet," Seamus explained.

"Why must we be discreet, as you say? You are part of the family."

"I am still only an adopted son. I am tolerated as long as I am perceived to be harmless. I am a bachelor and you are a maiden, so we may not be seen around town alone together again. It would ruin you."

"But we have been seen, *non?*"

"I think your father plans to dismiss it as cousinly friendliness, even naïveté. Now it would be best if you are not in my company, without a chaperone, in Town."

"I do not think I will enjoy the Season. But it is my father and Beaujolais' wish."

"You will be a success, no doubt." He hoped he was remaining impartial on the outside, at least.

"But will I be happy?" she asked, looking skyward.

"I hope so. I would advise you to keep Society in perspective. It can be a very fickle thing, I hear. However, having a duke for a father and Ashbury for a *grandpère* will help tremendously."

"I expect so. I think it may be a mixed blessing," she answered in a considering tone—wisely, he thought.

CHAPTER 15

*Y*ou are doing quite well. You are a natural horsewoman," Yardley said as he led her on a golden pony in a circle.

"False flattery!" Christelle had released her death grip on the reins at the very least. "Who knows, by this time next year I might graduate beyond the paddock."

He made a deep, hearty, rumbling sound. "Nonsense. I will have you on a blood mare by this time next week, when we arrive in London."

"So soon?" When she had arrived at Yardley, they had discussed staying on in the country for some time.

"The ladies think it is necessary to quell any possible rumours before they begin. People do tend to rusticate in the country when they have something to hide."

"I am perfectly happy to rusticate," she muttered.

"We will again, in time," he reassured her. "However, we must go with the social whirl until the fuss dies down."

"Fuss is not a good word in my book."

"Nor in mine, but it must be done, and the longer we put it off, the worse it will be."

He put his fingers to his lips and let out a loud whistle.

A beautiful black stallion came prancing out from the stables, stopped and looked expectantly at her father. He began to lead her pony by the bridle and handed it into the charge of a groom. Christelle had fully expected one of the grooms could teach her to ride as well as the Duke, but he had insisted on doing all of it himself. She was grateful for the time with him.

"Are we finished?"

"With the paddock." His voice indicated there was something more.

Another groom led out a white horse, who looked as if she were toying with the black stallion. Christelle had a sinking feeling that he expected her to ride one of these beasts.

He helped her down from the pony and then led her to the white mare. "This is Dido. And that is Hector."

"I am not ready, Papa," she protested as he took her hand and put it up to greet the horse.

"No one who is wise ever thinks they are ready the first time. But there must be a first time. You are quite ready. You will find no better trained horses than these. Dido knows the way and she will follow alongside Hector. You must trust me."

How could she refute such an ultimatum? "Very well." She took a deep breath and was hoisted atop the horse.

He mounted Hector and began to lead them out.

"Relax," he instructed. "Horses can sense you are nervous. The worst thing you can do is be frightened."

"How can I help how I feel? I am terrified!" She was afraid she had shouted.

He laughed at her. "That's the spirit. I was beginning to wonder if I had a clandestine affair in my past I did not remember. I could not imagine Lillian and I had produced a passive daughter."

"That is unkind, Papa."

"My apologies. But you must admit you have been very quiet."

"Who has a moment to speak here? I prefer to speak when I may be heard."

"You are wise beyond your years, my dear. If you are not careful, you will dispel all of the myths about young girls at their come outs. You might find yourself hooking some hard to catch fish on your line."

"Whatever do you mean?"

"It is unfashionable to have too much wit or wisdom at your age. The *ton* prefers its young ladies to be guileless and innocent."

"You are jesting, surely."

"I am afraid not. However, what they do not realize is the more intelligent men do not always agree. Certainly the rogues do not, but they stay away from the new crop."

"What a strange country this is."

"Do you see? You have walked Dido across the meadow with no harm."

By Jove, she had. She had not even realized. "You distracted me."

"Only to prove a point. When you are calm and in command, the horse will do as it is trained to do. Never panic on a horse. Always be firm. Now, shall we attempt a canter back to the stables?"

"I suppose we may if you insist."

"There is nothing to fear. I can stop her if you lose control."

She met his eyes and knew he told the truth. *Trust him.* She closed her eyes and nodded.

"That's my girl. Now click your tongue and release the reins a little."

She did as he said and held her breath while her mind was instructing her to relax.

"Now a nudge with your leg or your whip. Excellent."

The horse picked up its momentum and she felt for the first time the exhilaration of speed. Christelle felt free and giddy until she considered she would have to stop. She made the mistake of looking at the wooden railing ahead.

She should not have worried. When they approached the fence the horse naturally slowed, even before she remembered she was supposed to pull on the bit.

She looked over at her father as she finally dared to take a breath. He was beaming proudly at her.

"You have an excellent seat. And I do not say that because I took part in creating it."

"Thank you, Papa." She cast him a wry grin.

"Excellent, Christelle!" Beaujolais called as she came towards the stables. "You may be ready yet for Hyde Park this Season," she exclaimed.

"I think so, too. Of course, Dido is an excellent horse for your first canter," Yardley said with a smile.

"She is." Beaujolais rubbed the horse's forehead and neck affectionately. "Are you ready to go, girl?"

Dido nickered at her owner in acknowledgement.

Yardley assisted Christelle to dismount from the horse and then boosted Beaujolais into the saddle. Every afternoon they went out on a ride together, it seemed.

"The others are waiting for you in the saloon," Beaujolais said to Christelle. "Remember I told you Monsieur St. Pierre has been engaged to ensure Maili is ready for the London ballroom? He has arrived, so why do you not join them?"

Christelle had discussed this with Lady Ashbury, but they had decided they could never be too prepared. The French took dancing very seriously—it was an art, an expression. Christelle knew the steps to these dances in her dreams.

Seamus had a sinking feeling in the pit of his stomach as he donned his breeches and top boots for the journey home. He could not say why, but he felt as if he was leaving the Christelle he cared for behind. It was a melodramatic sentiment, of course. He would see her at family gatherings. Yet at those gatherings she would very likely be the centre of attention or, before long, bear someone else's name. It was the first time he had ever wished he had wealth and a title, and he hated the fact that he had the thought.

He looked back over the room. His few belongings were already packed. He made his way down the stairs to say his goodbyes.

He heard the strains of the piano echoing through the house and moved towards the sound.

"*Magnifique, mademoiselle!*" he heard a heavily accented French voice say.

"Where did you learn to dance like that?" Maili asked Christelle. Approaching the ballroom, Seamus watched them from the doorway.

"It is the way they teach it in Paris. Lose yourself in the music," Christelle said.

"I think losing herself in the music is the problem," Lady Ashbury said.

"She is very free spirited, this one. Let us try the waltz. But remember, you must receive the permission before dancing it in London," Monsieur instructed.

Lady Ashbury began to play the notes to the Viennese waltz, and the dancing master took Maili in hand as Christelle stood by to watch.

Seamus could not very well interrupt at this moment. He was in his riding boots. Nonetheless, he could not miss this opportunity. He strode quietly to Christelle and held out his hand.

"*Madamoiselle* Christelle, may I have this dance?"

Her eyes brightened and she looked up at him with a radiant smile. "*Oui, je serais enchanté.*"

It was all he needed to hear before he swept her into the timing of the dance.

Seamus had learned to dance, being a part of the Ashbury family. They did love their music and dancing. This was perhaps the first time he was grateful for it.

He tried to memorize everything about Christelle, knowing it may be the last time he would have the freedom to do so. Even if he were fortunate enough to secure a dance with her in London, it would be under the watchful eyes of Society.

Her dainty hands seared his palm with fire. His hand encircled her waist, and it took a great deal of restraint not to pull her in closer. He closed his eyes and allowed his senses to capture the moment; to inhale her scent of jasmine, but not for too long. He wanted to see her.

Seamus looked down and found those golden eyes were watching him just as intently. The couple continued to float through the air as they stepped and twirled. There was nothing and no one else in the room but them.

If only time could stand still.

When the music drew to a close and they stopped, it was a few moments before he could draw his eyes from hers. They looked up to see the others staring at them in dismay—or what he perceived to be dismay. Had he lost himself to all propriety? He would not trust himself in Town with her.

Monsieur St. Pierre wiped a tear away and began to clap. "*Si beau! Parfait!*"

Lady Ashbury sat quietly, and Maili looked astonished.

"I came to say my farewells. I must return to Town."

"So soon?" Christelle asked with a slight frown.

"I will see you in London. Remember what I told you," he said quietly.

"*Oui,*" she whispered. "I will not forget."

He received an exuberant hug from his sister and walked to the pianoforte to kiss Lady Ashbury's hand.

"Be careful," she warned. She gave him a look that held pity, and he suspected her words were less to do with his journey than his feelings for Christelle.

He bid the rest of the party *adieu*, and set out on his trusty steed, feeling very much as though he had just left happiness behind.

CHAPTER 16

*C*hristelle was returning to London, but this time she was as far from being the pauper she had been just a few weeks ago as it was possible to be. It was difficult to believe. Her new family was kindness itself, but she still felt she was a foreigner. As they passed through the streets towards the luxurious realm of Mayfair, she realized her future was still as unknown as the day the stagecoach had left her on the steps of The White Bear. At least she would not be facing that future alone—although it would be just as frightening—but with her father by her side.

She refused to dwell on what she had missed and instead live for each day. However, she still did not find it comfortable to be amongst a large, ebullient clan.

Even now, her time was not her own. Her days were filled before the Season had begun, it seemed. There was to be a grand ball in her honour to open the Season, which in itself was enough to make her ill. Afterwards, there were morning calls, Venetian breakfasts, dances at Almack's, balls, the theatre, Vauxhall, and rides in the park to look forward to, she was frequently told. But first, there would be more fittings with Madame Monique. The modiste normally made private calls for fittings for someone so grand, but Christelle wanted to visit and see all her fellow seamstresses again.

The Duchess had decided it would be simplest for Maili, along with Lord and Lady Craig, to stay together at Yardley Court for the Season. The girls would be attending the same functions, and could therefore be chaperoned together.

Christelle was happy to finally reach her apartments, which had quickly become a refuge. The coverlet and draperies were a soft rose hue, and a pale green paper with tiny roses covered the wall. She lay flat, staring up at the floral pattern in the canopy and wondering why she could not be more like her cousin. She adored Maili, but was exhausted by her exuberance. Why could they not share that?

She rested in blissful peace for a while before a maid came to inform her the carriage was waiting to convey her to the modiste.

Lady Craig was to accompany them to help Maili with her choices, and Christelle had even drawn up some sketches she thought would flatter her cousin.

It was comforting to alight in front of the shop, and hear the familiar ringing of the bell when the door opened. Madame immediately came into the salon and curtseyed deferentially to them.

"*Bonjour*, Madame," Christelle said familiarly. "I assume you know Lady Craig? This is my cousin, Miss Maili Craig. She would like to have some gowns made as well."

"*Oui*, of course. There are pattern books here for your perusal. These are the more appropriate for a young lady making her come out." Madame directed them to one book in particular. "I will bring some fabrics I think would complement your colouring." Maili and Lady Craig went to peruse the sketches and Christelle looked expectantly at Madame. "May I please see the girls? Am I not to have fittings?"

Madame opened her mouth as if to protest but reluctantly nodded her head. She went through into the workroom. A few of the girls looked up at her and smiled, but most kept their eyes on their work.

Christelle sought out Noelle and Lorena, but they did not look at her. No matter how long she considered them, they would not meet her gaze. She was not comfortable speaking out to them in front of everyone.

"Perhaps it would be best if we did the fittings at Yardley Court after all," Madame said quietly.

Christelle nodded and turned back to the salon before she became upset. Why would they not look at her? It hurt deep inside to discover their friendship was not real. Could Madame have warned them away? It made no sense.

"I have some sketches for my cousin," Christelle remarked as they perused Maili's choices. She took them from the leather satchel she had brought them in. She was too sad to be excited for Maili, and she felt horrid about it. Yet, she could not put aside the knowledge that the two people she had been closest to—had shared a room with— would not even look at her. True, it had only been for a short time, but could they not be even a little bit happy for her?

Would Society be any less fickle? She doubted it. She had already seen the evidence before her own eyes of how people pandered to the wealthy and titled.

"*Naturellement*, those colours that are best for you a young made-moiselle cannot wear. Black and darker colours must not be done. We must try the cream, silver, lighter greens and such."

"But I will look washed out!" Maili protested.

"Nonsense. Not in a Monique gown. Your cousin, she has made several patterns which will suit you very well indeed. A nice design and fit draws attention to you, not the fabric. *Non?*"

Margaux nodded to Maili. Christelle remained quiet. She had done her part.

"Very well. I shall have these made up and send word when they are ready for fittings."

"*Merci*, Madame," Christelle said, trying to mask her sadness. Madame gave her a sympathetic look and walked her to the door.

"They do not know what to think, *chérie*. And are perhaps a little jealous. When they understand you are the same in here," she pointed to her chest, "they will do better."

They had seen the true her, and nothing had changed. If they could not remain her friends now and be happy for her, she had little hope for future relationships when people only knew her as Yardley's daughter.

If only it were as simple as asking Joseph to send for Dr. Craig and have him sort it all out for her. Yet here she sat in the carriage with his family, feeling the distance widen between them.

"Will all of the dresses be finished in time?" Maili asked.

"They work seven days a week to make certain," Christelle answered.

"Seven?"

"Each girl has an afternoon off a week."

"I did not realize. Are they paid well? I suppose it is gauche to ask," Maili said with dismay.

"I imagine one ball gown is more than a year's wages for them." Lady Craig looked at Christelle.

"*Oui*. But Madame does treat them well."

"A small consolation. I may not enjoy the gowns as much." Maili frowned.

"They are necessary, Maili. It provides them with work," Margaux explained.

"I did not begrudge the patrons while I was there," Christelle said with a smile.

Maili had a furrowed brow and did not appear to be convinced.

"Where does Seamus live?" she asked after they had passed the shops in Bond Street.

"I believe in St. James's," Lady Craig replied.

"May we drive by?"

"I do not see why not. We can also drive by Charing Cross Hospital, which is not far." Margaux opened the hatch to redirect the driver.

"I hope he will come to dinner soon. I do wish he could stay with us during the Season," Maili remarked.

Christelle's heart lurched at the thought.

"He would be welcome, of course," Lady Craig said. "Perhaps, if Jolie asked, he might consider doing so. Seamus is not the typical bachelor who finds it necessary to keep separate quarters."

No, he is not, Christelle thought fondly to herself. As they passed his apartments, she realized just how much she had missed him, though it had only been ten days since she had waltzed with him.

~

The days were longer, the air was warmer, and the daffodils were blooming all over the park. People were lingering outside longer, and the *ton* was beginning to descend on Town for the Season, Seamus noticed as he walked towards White's to answer yet another summons from his family. Spring had sprung at last.

The inside of the club was crowded, much more so than the last time he had visited. The odour of cigar and aristocrat was mixed with the gentle drone of conversation. He found Lord Ashbury along with His Grace, the Duke of Yardley, Lord Harris and his father, Lord Craig. A formidable group they were, all together. They smiled at his approach and stood up to greet him.

Lord Ashbury waved his finger to request a drink for Seamus and indicated a vacant chair next to him for Seamus to sit down on.

"If only Charles were here," Lord Ashbury mused, "then we would be complete."

"Will they be arriving soon?" Lord Harris asked.

"It depends on the babe," Ashbury replied. "They have not yet decided. Sarah will not leave him in the country and he is still suffering from the colic."

Seamus almost laughed at these men who groaned in sympathy. If anyone had told him of this scenario a decade ago, he would have thought them candidates for Bedlam. He was mildly envious of these men and their families, however—if not of the colic.

The waiter placed a glass of brandy in front of him. He swirled the glass and took in the sweet fruity notes of the amber liquid before swallowing a relaxing sip of heat. Yardley discussed the available stock at Tattersall's, and Harris told them the results of the prize-fight between Jem Ward and some unknown challenger. Then, at last, they came to the point.

"We have a reason for asking you here, my son, other than your company, of course," Gavin said.

Seamus raised an enquiring brow.

"I dare say it is my turn to talk," Yardley put in, setting down his glass and clearing his throat. Seamus wondered if he should be concerned. He waited for the Duke to speak.

"It would appear the ladies of the family have put their heads together and decided they would prefer it if you stayed at Yardley Court for the Season."

Seamus stared silently, waiting for the hammer to fall. But it didn't.

"It will not increase your distance from the hospital, and your mother and I would dearly love to have the time with you while we are here," Gavin explained.

"It would not require you to give up your bachelorhood," Yardley said with a smirk.

"Though they do expect you to come the pretty with your sister and cousin," Harris added frankly.

"If it is too great an imposition, I am certain we can break it to them gently," Lord Ashbury said.

"I confess, I was expecting something serious with all of you here, as if I had been at fault somehow."

"So you will do it?"

"I do not have a good reason not to." Although the moment Seamus uttered the words, he realized Christelle would be there all the while. Selfishly, he was delighted and realistically, he was heartbroken.

"That is a relief," Yardley said, visibly relaxing. "We thought we might have to take you to a back alley in order to convince you."

"Oh, be sure to act surprised when they ask you," Ashbury reminded.

"I know Margaux and Beaujolais will be relieved to have help in chaperoning the girls.

Neither one of them is up to long nights in their condition."

"Anjou is not, either," Harris confessed. "It is a good thing you agreed."

"She is in a delicate condition as well?" Ashbury asked. "I am both delighted and terrified," he said with a huge grin. He held up his glass to congratulate Lord Harris.

"To my twelfth grandchild."

"Hear, hear." They all raised their glasses.

"Seamus, tell us of your prospects. Will you also be looking to settle down this Season? Or did I imagine overhearing that?" Yardley asked as he finished the last sip of his drink and set the glass down.

Seamus swallowed hard. "I would not be opposed to it, sir."

He would swear Harris was laughing at him. The big seaman's shoulders were shaking, he was convinced.

"Your *grandmère* will have her hands full this Season, I can see." Ashbury chuckled.

"Indeed, if you find someone of interest, I will be happy to make introductions," Yardley offered with an amused look.

"You are too kind," Seamus retorted to the laughter of the men.

"I still intend to do something for you, like it or not," Yardley insisted.

"I assure you, it is not necessary."

"You know, my son, there is always the unentailed estate near Edinburgh. You are verra welcome to it. I know the university would welcome you if you wanted to continue with Medicine, although the estate would more than adequately provide a gentleman's living."

"Thank you, but I still enjoy Medicine as I know you do. I have been more than busy since a certain grandfather put the word out."

"I cannot think what you mean," Ashbury said, his cheeks taking on a slight pink hue.

"I suppose we had best return for dinner. We are charged with bringing you with us, Seamus."

"It requires all four of you?" He eyed them sceptically.

"I suppose we cannot avoid returning to the house for the entire Season," Ashbury confessed sheepishly.

"No," Yardley agreed. "But we can stay far away from the callers and modistes!"

"Harris, stop looking smug over there. You will have your chance," Gavin warned.

"There is no smugness behind this grin, I assure you. However, I have no doubt my boys will be the Terrors of London when their time comes."

"I would rather that than daughters. On the Marriage Mart, anyway," Ashbury added. "I never thought I would marry off my girls." He gave them all a half-sympathetic, half-devilish look before leading the way out.

CHAPTER 17

*W*hirl was an understatement. In fact, it was a massively inaccurate description for complete and utter chaos. The house had been at sixes and sevens for several days, now. Christelle felt a mere spectator, as if she had been watching things happen to her and around her, rather than participating.

Three *enceinte* Ashbury sisters, along with their mother, were a force to be reckoned with—or not to reckon with, as Christelle preferred. She stayed out of the way.

Flowers made Margaux cry; Anjou ran from the room looking green several times each day, and Beaujolais changed her mind as often about menus and music. The nursery was relative calm in comparison.

Occasionally, Maili would dive into the foray, but she could laugh about all of it with anticipatory excitement.

The one thing Christelle did look forward to was having Seamus here. He would be moving into the house for the Season. She was not certain why. If she were he, she would much prefer to be living in his rooms, but perhaps he enjoyed being around his family. Lots and lots of family.

It was not that she was unused to being around people, it was more the unfamiliarity with her role and this new identity which unnerved her.

There were two more hours until her introductory dinner, to which Beaujolais had invited thirty-nine intimate friends in addition to the eleven adult family members present. Christelle was not certain she even knew thirty-nine people.

Sybil was ready to help her dress and complete her toilette. Christelle was very proud of her gown—and Maili's—for they were both of her design. She had chosen a pale blue silk with an organza overdress so the skirt and sleeves would flow about her when she danced. The bodice had been appliquéd with a pattern of tiny pearls to match her necklace. Sybil braided her hair in a circlet and placed small white camellia buds in some of the criss-crosses and secured them with pins.

Christelle placed her mother's pearls about her neck, and attached the matching earrings given to her by her father for her birthday. He had offered her any of the family jewels for this night, but she was more comfortable with simple embellishment.

The ring! She had not thought to give the ring back to her father. It must be his. She dismissed Sybil and went to search her trunk until she found the small stuffed doll she stored it in. She pried open the stitches and fished around for the ring.

Having located it, she went out to the hall and started towards her father's study. Perhaps he was still dressing. Christelle paused in front of his apartments. She was still too uncomfortable to knock on his door. She searched the hallway until she found a servant to do it for her.

"His Grace says you may go to his dressing room now, or await him in his study."

The man bowed and continued on with his—no doubt—numerous duties on a night such as this.

Why was she more nervous to go to her father's room than dance at the ball? She was only three doors away. She held up her head and knocked. No matter what she was feeling inside, she would behave with dignity, poise and grace on the outside.

"Christelle, you look beautiful beyond words," her father said when she was shown in. His valet was helping him into his coat. He was an extremely handsome man, especially when he smiled. They shared the same golden hair and tawny eyes, and his were twinkling back at her. He was dressed in grey breeches and a blue waistcoat which matched her dress.

"Am I not supposed to fetch you from your rooms? I am unused to having a female ready before me," he laughed.

"And I am unused to having an army of servants to wait upon me," she replied.

The valet held out a long piece of cloth and waited for the Duke to be silent.

Christelle could see the man was becoming flustered. "I shall wait here until..."

"Rogers," the man supplied.

"...Rogers is finished."

The man gave her an appreciative glance and began his master-piece around the Duke's neck. It was rather fascinating. Christelle had never seen a neckcloth tied before. He finished by placing an onyx pin through the folds.

"Is there something you wish to discuss, or did you come to learn about the male *toilette*?" Yardley gave a suspicious look to the valet, who was picking imaginary lint from his coat.

"That will do, Rogers. Impeccable as always." The man bowed and left the room with a barely perceptible click of the latch.

"Are you nervous?" he asked, giving Christelle a gentle glance. "You need not be. We have every dance arranged for you until supper. By then, I am certain your remaining dances will be spoken for. If not, your uncles will be waiting."

"I had not considered the necessity. I do believe I am ready to have done with this ball. There has been so much fuss and I do not like being the cause."

He took her hand and looked her in the eye. "Never fear, if it was not for you, they would create some other reason to cause a fuss. One learns to let them be." He smiled, his eyes twinkling.

"Are you ready to go to dinner? It will be fifty of your closest friends to prepare you for the remainder of the evening," he said dryly.

"*Oui.* I am ready. But first, I wanted to return this to you. I believe it is yours, *non?*"

She opened her hand it to reveal the large onyx ring, which was a perfect match to the pin gracing his neckcloth.

"Where did you find this? It has been missing since my father's death."

The look on his face almost caused her to weep. Her throat burned as she watched him wrestle with his own emotions.

"It was sewn inside my childhood doll. I found it in the bottom of my mother's trunk," she answered quietly. She dared not say her mother's name in the presence of anyone in the house.

"Of course. Lillian. Thank you for returning it to me. Let me say, however, I am far more pleased to have you here."

He placed the ring on his finger and he held out his arm to escort her. They walked to the next room to collect Beaujolais and made their way to greet the guests.

Only a few more blessed minutes, she thought, until she would see him again...

...Except he was not there. His seat at the dinner table was empty. Lord Craig conveyed his excuses. The disappointment Christelle felt at Dr. Craig's absence dimmed the splendour of the occasion; and it was all for her. Well, for Maili and her, she thought guiltily. She had been so concerned about her own plight with this entry into the unknown world of London Society, she had scarcely considered how Maili was faring. She should not have worried. The girl was a light unto herself, shining with excitement and already gathering a court of admirers, by the looks of it. Christelle had designed a gown of pale green linen to complement her cousin's auburn locks and grey eyes, so similar to her brother's. An ivory overdress with ivory gloves and a pearl necklace enhanced her peaches-and-cream complexion.

The ballroom was exquisitely decorated with floral arrangements in pastel hues, which caused Christelle to smile. Her father had cared enough to mention it. She could not think that detail was a coincidence.

One wall of the ballroom was lined with mirrors and the other with gilded chairs. Crystal chandeliers hung from the painted ceiling and glistened with candlelight. The orchestra was poised and ready to perform on a dais at the end of the room. It was other-worldly to Christelle, the stuff one read of in fairy tales or dreamed of alone in bed at night while staving off loneliness.

She stood in the receiving line between her father and Beaujolais, greeting each guest and watching them attempt to mask their curiosity when they caught the first glimpse of her. It was amusing and horrifying at the same time.

"I do not think a single invitation went unaccepted. It will be a crush tonight," Beaujolais said in her ear during a pause between guests.

"Perhaps some will leave when they see the crowd," Christelle replied.

"No chance of that," her father said, sounding amused. "Do not be fooled. A crush means success to a London hostess. Besides, they all want to know who you are."

"Yes, indeed. I did not mean it was a bad thing. There is plenty of room on the terrace and in the card-rooms," Beaujolais said with a laugh. "Oh, here is Cavenray."

"My dear, allow me to introduce His Grace, the Duke of Cavenray. Your Grace, may I present my daughter, Lady Christelle Stanton."

A clichéd tall, dark and handsome man looked at her lazily from beneath hooded eyelids, though she could see the gleam in his eye was keen as he studied her. He was dressed simply but elegantly, all in black save for his crisp white neckcloth. "Charmed," he drawled. "May I beg the honour of reserving a set with you this evening, my lady?"

"I would be delighted, sir. Perhaps the cotillion?" She suggested her first open dance.

He bowed before moving on to his introduction of Maili and the rest of the party.

"He has been the most elusive bachelor for the past five years, ever since he came into his title," Beaujolais informed her discreetly.

Christelle could not see why. He clearly held himself in high esteem, yet were he plain Mr. Cavenray, she doubted anyone would think him a greater catch than the next man. Although, in fairness, she granted him the acknowledgement he was handsome, in a devilish kind of way.

She did not particularly want to dance with the Duke. There was really only one person, other than her father, whom she wished to dance with tonight. He still had not arrived.

The receiving line broke up and the music began. Yardley danced the opening quadrille with her, and Lord Craig danced it with Maili. It had been planned with military precision. The high-ranking gentlemen of the family—the uncles and grandfather—were to dance the first four dances with them. It would ensure their place in society and allow them time to grow comfortable with the situation. Once her promised dances were finished, Christelle looked for Seamus after every dance before she accepted any other partner.

After her four safe dances with her family, the Duke of Cavenray was waiting near Beaujolais to claim Christelle's hand. She was indescribably nervous around him, and knew this quintessential English aristocrat would expect poise, wit and other such nonsense. Unless she misjudged the matter, he was used to, and expected, flattery.

Fortunately, the cotillion was a dance she could perform with little thought. The Duke surprised her by speaking first, though he drawled in lazy tones.

"Did I hear you are recently arrived from Paris?"

"Yes, Your Grace," she replied meekly, unwilling to answer with more than was asked for, for fear every word was being measured.

"I hope you find London meets your standards," he said less haughtily, as if he had a script for dances.

"Ah, but my standards mean very little, sir, when one considers from where I have come. I have no other standard to measure it by than Paris. And even then, very little of Paris."

"Very well. I shall rephrase," he said, looking mildly amused. It was the first show of character she had seen from him. "Do you enjoy London? Or England, for that matter?"

She had time to consider her answer as the movement of the dance separated them and she was partnered with someone else for a few bars.

"I enjoyed my time in the country very much, sir. And I have enjoyed some things about London."

"A diplomatic answer, though unflattering. I do hope my place of birth will gain favour in your estimation before long. You must allow me to show some of it to you. Perhaps a ride in the park?"

"I shall look forward to it, Your Grace," she answered demurely.

Maili passed by with her partner, behaving a bit too exuberantly. She looked flushed and was laughing, causing the Duke to look sideways at her beneath his lids. Christelle thought she sensed disapproval, but the look was gone before she could decide.

"Your cousin?" he enquired.

"Maili? Yes. She has a certain zest for life."

"Yes, zest. An apt description." He had returned to the bored, cultured tone.

The set drew to a close and he led her back to Beaujolais.

"Your servant," he said with a punctilious bow. He then walked away, leaving her feeling as if he were some type of enigma. She had to stop herself from shivering. There was likely more to the man than the veneer he wore.

Christelle escaped briefly to the retiring room and overheard a commotion at the front entrance as she descended the stairs. She stopped at the doorway to see what was the matter.

"I assure you, I am welcome here," a voice declared in calm but annoyed tones.

"Yet you do not have an invitation, sir. I have strict orders," Childers said in stiff, military accents.

The voice was oddly familiar... Christelle walked closer. "Mr. Cole!"

"My lady." He bowed, his relief evident.

"It is all right, Childers." The butler bowed and stepped aside, although his reluctance was clear.

She knew very little about unwritten social codes, but was certain she would be schooled on them later, to judge by the look of mortification on Childers' face. But this was her ball, and Mr. Cole had shown her exceeding kindness, as had Dr. Craig. If they had not, she might not have been in the ballroom tonight.

"How did you find me?" she asked. She gazed at him with surprise.

"I could not imagine there was more than one Christelle newly arrived to London. All the buzz in the clubs is about you, you know."

No, she had not known.

"Are all of your dances spoken for? Dare I ask?"

She looked around the ballroom hopefully, but there was still no sign of Dr. Craig. "My partner for this dance has not arrived. I would be pleased to dance it with you instead," she answered graciously.

They joined the nearest set and she observed Mr. Cole more closely than she had during their first encounter, when she had been too overwhelmed to notice details. He was certainly at home amongst this crowd. He was dressed elegantly; in fact, he would be at home in a Parisian ballroom. He wore golden breeches with a gold coat and a cream-coloured, embroidered waistcoat, the latter also embellished with fobs and chains. His intricate neck-cloth was foaming with lace. He wore dancing pumps to match. Even so, he was only a few inches above her height.

"I did not expect to find you in such a grand place. Imagine my surprise when I arrived to hear the news."

"Nor did I know such privilege would be mine when I met you in Dover." She smiled sheepishly.

"There was no need to work as a seamstress, after all."

"I did not realize who my father was when I arrived. I did spend some time as a seamstress before I found him."

"A true fairytale, then." His eyes had a strange gleam, though he was smiling as he took her hand.

"And you have been fortunate enough to find you belong to two of the most illustrious houses in all of England."

"Yes, they have been very kind and welcoming."

"A blessed turn of events."

"And what of yourself? May I enquire what brings you back to London so soon?" She found she was genuinely curious.

He looked solemn, and for a moment she did not think he would answer. "I have returned to seek another posting. My uncle was unfortunate in his choice of acquaintances and it is still difficult to overcome the effects of sharing his name at times... but I say too much."

"I did ask. I apologize—and I am sorry you are suffering."

"Working for the Foreign Office has provided respite, for the most part. But I darken your evening. Let us speak of something joyous."

"I have gained more family than I ever could have hoped. My cousin also makes her come out tonight," Christelle said, indicating Maili with a tilt of her head.

"May I have an introduction to her after our dance?"

"Yes, of course. She is my cousin from Scotland, Miss Craig."

"That explains why I was unaware of her. She is enchanting," Mr. Cole said as he glanced at Maili.

The dance ended and Mr.Cole led Christelle towards her family, where Maili's partner was returning her to Lady Craig. Christelle performed the introductions and Maili was immediately swept back onto the floor by Mr. Cole.

CHAPTER 18

*T*his could not be happening. Seamus looked with frustration at the clock. Today of all days, he could not be late. He had not even arrived home at a decent hour, to enable him to pack his belongings and move into Yardley Court. Now, it appeared he was going to miss dinner before the ball which would introduce Christelle and Maili to Society.

At least he'd had the forethought to send over his trunks this morning, along with flowers for Christelle and his sister.

Yet this inconvenience was part of his life as a physician—unless he stopped caring for patients and devoted himself to teaching and research. It was simply impossible in London, for there were more patients than decent, safe doctors to help. He was caught in a difficult situation. With such a desperate need for more physicians, teaching was the best thing he could do for the profession.

As he was packing up his belongings to leave early for the day, his secretary handed him a note Mrs. Baker had sent, asking him to come post-haste. There was something wrong with Mr. Baker. It must be bad indeed for her to request a house call, which were difficult in a large city. By the time a doctor made it through all the traffic to a patient's house, it could be too late. There had to be a better way. With a sinking feeling, Seamus alighted from the conveyance outside the bakery and paid off the driver. He opened the door to the shop and proceeded up the stairs without waiting to be shown in.

Mrs. Baker came out from the bedroom as soon as she heard him, and the frightened look on her face did not give comfort.

"What has happened?"

"Oh, Dr. Craig, he sounds like a drowning rat. He hasn't been able to catch his breath and he keeps balling up his fist over his chest and groaning in pain."

"Show me to him," Seamus ordered.

He could hear what Mrs. Baker had described of her husband's suffering before he saw him. He placed his bag on the bed beside Mr. Baker and pulled back the old man's coverings to look more closely.

"How long has he been this way?"

"He woke up feeling very poorly. I sent him back to bed, and when I came to check how he did this afternoon, he was like this."

"So, several hours."

"Yes," she looked down guiltily. "I did not know today was different. He has had trouble for years."

"You could not know." Seamus examined him and feared the worst. It looked as if the man had had a severe heart spasm and would not live through the night. His hands and feet were already mottled and he was gasping for air.

He searched through his bag for some tincture of dandelion to try to alleviate the fluid on his lungs, but he knew it was fruitless. However, it was important for Mrs. Baker to feel as though everything had been done. He added some laudanum to make her husband more comfortable.

"He is not going to get better, is he?" she asked, her lower lip trembling.

"I do not believe so," Seamus said softly as his eyes met hers.

She nodded bravely, and pulling up a chair next to Mr. Baker took his hand.

Seamus did the same. He could not very well run off and join in the gaiety of a ball when Mr. Baker lay there dying.

"Is he in pain?"

"I do not believe so." Seamus used to hesitate when people would ask him that question. There was no way he could truly know what the man felt, but the more he learned, the more he suspected that there was no blood flow to the mind.

He did not know how long he sat there waiting for Mr. Baker to die. He tried not to think about what he was missing with Christelle, and wondering if she would even notice his absence. He would try to arrive in time for a dance if he could.

It was half past eleven when the man breathed his last. He did not know what to do with Mrs. Baker, although she looked exhausted. He confirmed that Mr. Baker was dead with a last check for a pulse and a breath, then gave a slight nod of his head to the widow.

He embraced Mrs. Baker and allowed her to weep on his shoulder.

"I am sorry I did not help him more," he said quietly in her ear.

"You did. I think we found you too late. I thank you for everything you did."

He gave her a sleeping draught and saw her to bed before letting himself out. He climbed into a hack on a night when he would rather walk alone and weep a little himself. He would never grow accustomed to this. To death. To failure.

He allowed himself a few moments of grief before putting on the mask of indifference so many in this profession had to don in order to endure it.

The hackney could not even get close to Yardley Court for all of the carriages lining the streets in wait. He was deposited two streets away and passed multiple servants lingering about. Some were entertaining themselves by dancing while they waited for their masters to call for them at the end of the night. Seamus sneaked in through the servants' entrance and was directed to his room.

Lord Craig's man was there, waiting for him. His father must have known. Medicine had been his life, too. As the valet helped him to dress quickly, he wondered if he could give it all up as Gavin had done. He was still able to practice Medicine on occasion. It was Seamus' life, but tonight had been a perfect example of his profession being opposed to his heart's desire.

Leaving his room, he heard the sounds of the orchestra growing stronger as he made his way to the ballroom. He paused at the top of the stairs to get oriented. It only took him seconds to find her. There was no one else in the room for him when she was there. She was dancing with someone he did not recognize, and his chest clenched with unfounded, uncharacteristic jealousy. He wanted to be that man, yet he had not even been here for her début.

He forced his eyes away so he would not be caught staring. He found his parents standing with the Duke and Duchess, and joined them.

"Forgive my tardiness," he said with a bow, trying to steel himself to do so, but he could not find the words to explain.

Gavin reached out and placed his hand on Seamus's sleeve and looked him in the eye. He was forced to look away to control himself. This was not the place.

"Mr. Baker?" he whispered. Seamus gave a slight inclination of his head.

"I am sorry, my son. It never gets easier."

Seamus took a deep breath and forced a smile. "Am I too late for a dance?"

"You will have to ask her yourself," Yardley answered, and Seamus realized she must be standing behind him.

She looked more beautiful when close, if it was possible. About to stare at her like a green youth, he remembered his manners in time and bowed.

"Lady Christelle, is it too late to request a dance?"

She smiled at him and it made everything else seem inconsequential.

"I have been saving several dances for you," she said as she put her arm on his sleeve.

They began to walk to the floor.

"Saving them for me? I imagine you are turning partners away. Besides, it would not do to dance more than once on your come out," he said in a slightly mocking tone.

She laughed. "Perhaps. All evening I think to myself, 'If I see Dr. Craig, I will dance the next set with him.' Then, if I do not see you, I accept the person who asks. Of course, my father, uncles and *grand-père* have all had turns."

"That would not leave many open sets," Seamus remarked, calculating in his head.

"I think that was the point," she said with a twinkle in her eye.

"Who was the last fortunate gentleman? I have not seen him before; and now he dances with Maili, I see."

"A Mr. Cole. He helped me to find the stage in Dover and purchased a ticket for me. Was that not extremely handsome of him?"

Seamus had to stop himself from missing a step. "I beg your pardon?"

She frowned. "Have I done something wrong?"

He shook his head but did not say anything, grateful for the changing of partners in the dance. A man of Mr. Cole's age would not do such a thing unless he intended repayment or mistook her for someone or something. He could not have known who she was, could he? Seamus was too exhausted to think clearly and eventually ascribed it to Mr. Cole doing a good deed. Surely, he thought vaguely, nothing problematic could come of it now.

Seamus took Christelle's hand again.

"Is it unpardonably rude to ask why you were late?" she asked timidly.

Seamus looked at her with tenderness. "Of course not. It is I who should be begging your pardon and asking for forgiveness. May we wait until the ball is over and I will tell you everything? I assure you I wanted to be here." He did not want to ruin her night.

She cocked her head to the side. "Very well, if you insist. I am simply glad you did come after all."

~

The morning papers were full of the news, as expected. It was the juicy tidbit for all the gossiping tongues, in every corner of London. The drawing room was overflowing with callers, especially those bold enough to dare a visit on the merest acquaintance with Yardley or the family—all anxious for a glimpse of Lady Christelle Stanton. It was a real-life fairytale.

Too bad Yardley had no inclination to accept callers that day. Childers sent away dozens of disappointed suitors who had been too smug to attend yet another insipid ball, for no one had guessed what an *on-dit* awaited. None of the newspapers, announcing the glittering festivity at Yardley Place, had even intimated at the relationship of the young lady being brought out to its ducal owner. Never fear, the ink on the betting books was scarcely dry on the page before a new one was started by those unhappy gentlemen to bet on the lovely Lady Christelle. Several of the bets were speculation on the size of her dowry, or which confirmed bachelor would sink this Season.

Yes, the Season was in full swing, if the animated chatter in the clubs and calls was anything to go by.

Christelle was blissfully unaware of all of it.

The ball had been better than she had expected once Dr. Craig had arrived. It had been difficult to hide her disappointment before he had finally appeared, in time for the last dance. Looking exhausted and despondent, he had apologized but not explained, and she had presumed he did not wish to burden her with whatever was on his mind.

The dance had been very special to her, though he had seemed distant and sad. He had not been at all as charming and talkative as Mr. Cole, which must stem from the latter's work in diplomacy, she decided.

Dr. Craig was an elegant dancer for one so tall, and Christelle soon forgot she was in a ballroom full of people curious to have a glimpse of her, this long-lost, legitimate child of Yardley's. She had felt herself relax and enjoy his company as she had not been able to with any other partner that night.

The country dance brought them together occasionally, though not as often as a waltz would have done. She had only minded that she had to be separated from him at all. She had felt herself smiling and perhaps dancing the steps in a livelier manner than was English and proper. She had decided she would worry about it later, for, with him, she was simply Christelle again.

There had been a few other dances with gentlemen she could scarcely recall. None of it mattered much to her. She wanted to do this for her new family. After the ball, she had formed the intention of not making herself known about Town any more than necessary.

Today was the day she was to ride out with the Duke of Cavenray. Fortunately, he had extended the invitation to include Maili too.

They set out from Yardley Place in a landau, which allowed them to see and be seen. Christelle quickly realized that was the sole point of a promenade in Hyde Park at the fashionable hour. She was thankful for Maili's presence, for there were never any gaps in the conversation when her cousin was present. Maili was greeting everyone as old acquaintances, with a bit more exuberance, perhaps, than the *ton* considered appropriate. The gentlemen seemed to think her a great gun, and Christelle had not noticed anyone cut her directly, though she had also not seen any approving glances either.

She glanced over to see the Duke's reaction, and thought she detected amusement under the hooded lids. The landau pulled to a stop, which was not a very great movement since they had previously been travelling at the speed of a turtle.

"Afternoon, Cavenray, ladies," Mr. Cole said in a pleasant voice as he doffed his hat to them.

"Join us, Cole," Cavenray commanded, notwithstanding his lazy drawl.

Christelle wondered why people tolerated being directed in such a way, but Cole did as he was bid. Perhaps the Duke did not make unreasonable demands.

"I am much obliged to you for sharing the most charming company, Cavenray."

The Duke inclined his head. "We are bored. I am trusting you to provide some diversion, Cole."

"Alas, I know very little other than there is to be a concert at Vauxhall three nights hence."

"That is not news," the Duke agreed.

"What is Vauxhall?" Christelle asked, though she had heard the name mentioned by someone.

"Oh, it is said to be the most fantastic evening!" Maili exclaimed. "You arrive by boat, there are fireworks, there are dark romantic pathways you can get lost in, and they say the shaved ham is worth dying for," she said dreamily.

"Something did die for it," the Duke said quietly, though Maili heard him and cast him a glare.

Christelle wanted to laugh.

"Shall we see you there, then?" Mr. Cole asked Maili.

"I hope so, but I am not certain what our plans are."

Sir Anthony rode by on some 'high-steppers' according to Maili, and the conversation went in a direction Christelle had little interest in.

She smiled politely as the trio discussed the latest offerings at Tattersall's, and how Lord Roth's chestnuts were superior to Sir Anthony's greys. Maili appeared to hold her own with the men. Christelle longed to be back walking in the park with Dr. Craig, when things had been simpler. She had scarcely seen him since he left the country house.

They moved on and passed some women who Christelle suspected to be of her mother's former occupation. She noticed the coy glance one of them gave Mr. Cole and the look of comprehension that passed over the Duke's face.

"Are you going to introduce us to your friend?" Maili asked innocently.

Mr. Cole had the grace to blush. "I would not call her a friend."

"Oh. Ohhhh," Maili said with understanding. "Why is your lady-bird promenading about Hyde Park?" she asked in a loud whisper.

The Duke made a slight choking noise before he disguised it, and Christelle felt like laughing again, though it was not really funny, despite the irony of it all. She wondered if all of them knew about her mother and her occupation after she was no longer a duchess.

"My dear, a lady is not supposed to know of these things." Mr. Cole gently chided Maili.

"Why does everyone think females are stupid? And why should we pretend we cannot see what is right there, as bold as brass, in front of us?"

Mr. Cole looked stupefied; the Duke wore the same look of bored amusement.

"Oh, Christelle, look! Is that Uncle Yardley?" She waved to catch the rider's notice.

"Good afternoon, Christelle, Maili," her father greeted them as he pulled Dido up next to their carriage. "Cavenray." He tipped his hat to the Duke and eyed Mr. Cole suspiciously.

"Who is your friend? I have not had the pleasure of an introduction," he said with quiet indolence.

"Mr. Cole, may I present my father, the Duke of Yardley."

The man stood up and bowed properly, despite his high collar points, skin-tight coat and breeches seemingly melded to his legs. How different he was from Dr. Craig! Yardley inclined his head but did not smile.

"I trust you are enjoying your ride?" Mr. Cole asked with a pleasant smile. With a negligent air, he twirled a looking-glass hanging from a chain.

"I am." Dido threw back her head and showed the whites of her eyes at Mr. Cole. Christelle had never seen her behave in such a fashion. The man sat back down and leaned away as Dido began to snort at him.

Christelle sensed tension and spoke up to break the awkwardness.

"Are you in Town for long this time, sir? Mr. Cole is with the Foreign Office," she informed her father.

"Are you indeed?" Yardley asked as Dido kept fidgeting. "Where are you posted?" He barked a command at the horse and she stilled.

"I have been in Paris, but I am awaiting my next orders."

"How interesting," Yardley said, and Christelle was almost embarrassed for the manner in which her father was treating the man. Christelle had noticed he was different in manner to those outside their family. The Duke had an air about him which could be construed as haughty and stern. What had he been like in his youth? What had he been like with her mother before their falling out? It was difficult to reconcile what she knew of either of her parents with what she had heard each of them say about the other. It was likely she would never know the exact truth.

"Where is Hector?" Christelle questioned.

"He had his exercise earlier. My Duchess was not able to ride her today, so I am obliging her."

"I had best be on my way," Mr. Cole said somewhat nervously. Dido was still breathing down his neck and Yardley was doing nothing to stop her.

Dido turned towards Mr. Cole as he alighted and lifted her tail. To Christelle's horror, the mare proceeded to splash his shiny Hessian boots. She would swear an expletive passed his lips, though it was too faint to be certain.

"I am mortified, Mr. Cole! Is there anything I can do for you?" she asked. With every evidence of disgust, he was hurriedly wiping the yellowish fluid from his boots.

"I think perhaps relieving the mare of his presence would be in the best interest of everyone," Yardley remarked with calm indifference.

"Think nothing of it," Mr. Cole said with a forced smile. A crowd was beginning to gather.

"You are very generous, sir." She inclined her head as he walked away.

"Christelle, would you walk with me for a few moments? I promise to return you to the carriage shortly."

"Of course, Papa."

He dismounted from Dido and handed Christelle down. They

walked several paces away from the crowd, and Dido returned to her usual calm, aloof demeanour.

"He danced with you at the ball, did he not?" Yardley asked with his eyes narrowed upon the retreating figure of Mr. Cole.

"Papa, he was the man who helped me in Dover. I told Childers to admit him."

"He came uninvited and expected to be admitted to a duke's house? You have had no contact with him since Dover?"

Christelle shook her head, knowing her father was right, yet not knowing what else she could have done. She looked at him in dismay.

"Papa," she chastised. "The man helped me."

"I will happily repay him the cost of the ticket, Christelle. But what kind of man gives money to a female alone without some type of expectation?"

"But I offered to repay him, Papa," she insisted.

"Did you?" He cast a glance at her. "So, is he here seeking his repayment in a different manner?"

"He has asked no such thing," she said, affronted.

"Oh, my dear, but he has. He gained entry into my house uninvited, and therefore to the *ton*. That is not the way a gentleman behaves, regardless of his easy smile and manners."

She was too angry to reply.

"How did he know where to find you? In Dover, you were still uncertain of employment, let alone who your father was."

It was a valid point, she had to concede, but she could still not pardon his rudeness to Mr. Cole.

"Even Dido did not like the popinjay!" he added, stopping and looking down at Christelle. "I want you to have no further contact with that man. I will look into him and if I am wrong, I will admit as much. But until then, there is not to be a word, ride or dance with him. Do you understand? Meanwhile I will repay your debt to him with my gratitude, etcetera, and relieve him of his need to further prey on your kindness."

"Yes, Papa," she said quietly, though she did not care for this side of her father one bit. She could have lived oblivious to this streak in him quite happily.

"I must have a care for you, Christelle," he said quietly. "I have good reason to trust no one."

And now, she had to return to the landau and pretend she had not just had her first argument with her father.

CHAPTER 19

*I*t was Maili's coming out as well, and she looked as though she was walking on air lately. There had been almost as many bouquets of flowers delivered for Maili as Christelle, Margaux had said. She was always a happy, radiant girl that others felt drawn to —and this occasion was to be no different, it seemed. Seamus had been concerned she would be disappointed for many of the reasons he knew why he himself would not be considered worthy of Christelle. However, being sponsored by a duke and a marquess, and with a respectable dowry, would at least give her the opportunity to make a reasonable match.

It was Wednesday afternoon when Seamus walked into Yardley Court after attending Mr. Baker's graveside funeral. Dare he hope Christelle had saved Wednesday afternoon for him as before? Instead, he was to find her and Maili entertaining in the saloon, which was full of hopeful suitors. He looked into the room of Corinthianesque and dandified hopefuls and quickly backed away. Perhaps she might find some time for a walk in the garden with him later in the day. He would not bother trying to compete with that tomfoolery. Every day had been similar—she was riding, driving, making calls, being called upon...and that was just during the daytime. Every night there was a gala, ball, or soirée of some sort, and he was truly happy for her. It occurred to him it was probable she was not avoiding him on purpose. However, he realized with a pang, if this was the life she wished to lead, then he was not the husband for her.

He chose instead to escape to the billiard room, where he found Yardley, Harris and Gavin. He always had seemed to blend in better with the older crowd than the young bucks. He had never sown his wild oats, for he had never seen the purpose. Very likely, he thought, considering the matter, the time in the orphanage had given him an appreciation for what he had. He had never felt the need to debauch himself at every opportunity, especially when he daily saw the effects of such behaviour on his patients.

"Seamus, do come and join us," the men greeted him.

"Am I intruding?" he asked.

"I suppose you have seen the downstairs nursery?" Harris jested, handing him a cue.

"Aye. It made me feel quite elderly."

"The time is up for you, my lad. What you need, my boy, is a wife," Harris said as he struck his ball.

"I would have agreed with you before I came to London. It is why I came here, in fact. However, I feel married to my work of late," Seamus replied, hitting the red cue ball and sending it into the pocket.

All three men openly stared at him, though Gavin's eyes held empathy.

"The offer of the Edinburgh estate still stands," Gavin remarked.

"Thank you, but no. I am simply morose from the loss of a patient. And I have missed everything I was to attend on behalf of Maili and Christelle. It will pass."

Yardley handed him a glass of brandy. "If you had had the day I did with Christelle, you might rather be in hospital."

"Did something happen to her?" Seamus could not mask his concern.

"Merely fending off rogues. It is no different for any protective father, I suppose."

"I have no doubt she is much sought after," Seamus conceded with a sinking feeling inside.

"You would not believe the offers I have refused already," Yardley said with the shake of his head.

"Are they not respectable?" Seamus thought surely not.

"We have seen all varieties, I am afraid. I have never heard of this man, Cole. I have put my secretary on to it, of course, but there is something about him that bothers me."

"Who is he?" Harris asked.

"One Mr. Cole of the Foreign Office, or so he says. He apparently helped Christelle in Dover—even purchased her a ticket for the stage, which he would not allow her to repay—then had the effrontery to arrive for her coming out ball without an invitation. He used his so-called good deed as a way to wrestle his way in."

"How could he have known who she was? She did not know she was your daughter at the time of their chance meeting. Has he done anything else?" Seamus asked, though not sure he wanted the answer.

"Other than dance with her at the ball and then force an introduction in the park?"

Gavin and Harris made faces of distaste.

"Dido took a dislike to him and staled on his gleaming Hessians," Yardley said with some satisfaction. "I have forbidden Christelle to have further contact with him until I may investigate him, but she is quite angry with me. I could see the fire blazing from her eyes when I told her."

"Why would she defend him?" Gavin asked.

"She believes it was honourable of him to have purchased her ticket and helped her. I grant she was desperate, but she thinks I was rude beyond the pale."

Seamus stood there, quietly waiting his turn while the other men took their shots. He could only hope that if he must give Christelle up, it would be to someone worthy. However, he could not think of that roomful of young gentleman in the drawing room and feel any of them would measure up to his satisfaction, given their various fobs, snuffboxes and affectations—not to mention quantities of lace.

"We must make certain she is never alone. I do not want her merely accompanied by a female chaperone."

"I do think she might resent that, sir, though I understand your protectiveness," Seamus said meekly.

"Almost certainly she will. The trick is to make sure she never knows what we are doing," Yardley agreed without a flicker.

"You cannot think to escort her everywhere, Yardley," Harris said. "You may be a duke, but you will certainly be *de trop* if you are hanging on your daughter's sleeve."

"Who says I want her to be courted? I am in no hurry." He gave Harris an incredulous look which was met with a smirk. "We have just found each other, I think a bit of doting is understandable."

"Will you turn respectable suitors away?" Gavin asked.

"Does such a thing exist where one's daughter is concerned?" Yardley retorted.

Seamus felt distinctly uncomfortable and very, very disheartened.

"I would think forbidding anyone to court Maili would send her running straight into his arms," Gavin mused.

"Forbidden fruit is tastier," Harris agreed.

"Christelle seems mature for her age. She was quite blunt about her mother's occupation. I cannot think she would fall into the trap so easily," Yardley said, though it had obviously given him pause.

Seamus tended to agree that Christelle was wise beyond her years compared to Maili, who was as naïve as they came. However, Seamus knew how Christelle felt indebted towards himself, and if she felt similarly about Cole, there could be trouble.

"Now, how shall we divide up chaperoning my daughter?" Yardley asked with a mischievous grin.

"It will never work," Seamus said, though he could not believe the words had come from his lips.

"She will know you are spying on her and resent you," Harris concurred.

Yardley's face fell. "What do you suggest?"

"Someone nearer her own age," Harris suggested. "Meanwhile, I will ask around at the docks. Cole is bound to be familiar there if he travels frequently."

"I have already sent my secretary to make enquiries."

Seamus almost felt bad for the gentleman. He would not want the full force of Yardley and Harris looking into his past. Suddenly all of the men were staring at him.

"What is it?"

"Christelle is comfortable with you, Seamus. She would not suspect her cousin would be keeping an eye on her, especially since your sister will also be there."

"Sir, while I am flattered, I cannot abandon my new position. It would be a full-time task and then some to squire the two ladies everywhere."

"What if I hire you as my personal physician? Then you can continue your duties at the school and attend to the family."

"While I am honoured, I am sure, I am not ready to give up on my dreams of making Medicine a valid science of researched remedies and treatments."

The Duke studied him with uncomfortable intensity. Seamus would love nothing more than to spend every moment with Christelle —and even Maili. Could Yardley see his intentions and already found him lacking? Many people outside his immediate family thought he had windmills in his head when he began to speak about his profession and his aspirations. Employment was frowned upon by Society, even though a physician was a gentleman—just not the level of gentleman who would be worthy of a duke's daughter.

"May we compromise?" Yardley was not used to being told no.

"Sir, I do not know how. I have already missed the most important night of Maili and Christelle's début. I cannot choose between the responsibility and also my livelihood."

"May I speak to Seamus alone?" Gavin asked in his calm voice.

"Of course." Harris and Yardley placed their cue sticks in the wooden rack against the wall and left the room.

Seamus leaned on the edge of the table and Gavin sat down in a leather chair in front of him.

"You are not happy, my son."

"No." He closed his eyes. This was going to be one of those painfully introspective conversations he could not avoid. "I always grow so close to the patients. A loss of one is a deep blow."

Gavin sat for a moment and steepled his fingers in front of him. He was not one to be superfluous with words, but he gave great thought before he did speak.

"Perhaps your calling is in academia rather than in treatment."

"I cannot disagree with you. However, I could not support a family if I were to do such."

"This is where we differ. I would rather be caring for patients. Is accepting the estate abhorrent to you? Is it because you feel you must earn it yourself?"

"I suppose so." He was not sure why. It did not seem right to take from Iain's inheritance.

"It is no different from providing dowries for Catriona and Maili. I assure you, you will have to work the estate. It would not be as simple as you living there and being provided for."

Seamus felt pain in his throat. Was his father doing this so he might be more acceptable to Yardley? Seamus had hoped to buy his own estate one day, with his own hard-earned money.

"May I think on it?"

"You may, but the property has already been left to you. Whether you choose to take it over is up to you."

Seamus looked up in dismay. "I do not know what to say."

"I am proud of you, no matter what you decide to do. But if you love Christelle, I suggest taking Yardley up on this offer. You will not be likely to have another chance."

Gavin gave him a long, solemn look of empathy before leaving him alone with the burden of his choices. What should he do? Sell out for a chance with the woman he loved, or give her up because he could not yet give her the life she deserved?

$\sim$

Christelle sat on the cushioned window seat, looking out of the window from the sitting room of her apartments. There was so little time unoccupied—or alone for that matter—that she simply stared. She could not have told anyone what she saw, even had they asked her.

Maili came twirling into the room, holding two gowns.

"I do love the way this organza flows, but I love the way the sarsenet shimmers too. Which do you like?" She held up one, then the other.

Christelle pondered both gowns. "What is the occasion?"

"Vauxhall!" Maili could barely contain her excitement.

"Then I would say the organza. It will be too dark for anyone to appreciate shimmers."

"Excellent point. What will you wear?"

"I have not decided to go."

"But you must! It will be dream-like, and a break from all of the drab soirées with matrons in their horrid turbans staring down their noses and lorgnettes at us."

"I would love to see fireworks just once, but an evening at home is equally enticing. We have not been to bed before dawn in a week."

"And the Season has just begun!" Maili said this as if it were a good thing. She made Christelle feel like a dowager.

"Who would you like to dance with most? Cavenray or Weston? Perhaps Sir Anthony or Mr. Cole?" she asked as she waltzed with the lavender organza.

"I do not favour any one of them over the other. They are all very agreeable."

"Fustian! Cavenray is a cold fish, and Weston is handsome. I might enjoy kissing him at Vauxhall if I was to find myself lost on a dark walk. What about you?"

How could she tell Maili she had eyes only for her knight in shining armour? Maili's brother. Would Maili laugh at her?

Maili turned and looked at Christelle. "You must think me very silly. I suppose I am. Everyone thinks I do not remember what happened to my parents, or what it was like to live in the orphanage." She walked over and looked out of the window too. "But I do."

Christelle remained silent. She had thought Maili a little immature, perhaps, but she was no different from many of the girls who had been at school.

"It is simply that I *choose* to go on with my life and be happy rather than dwell in misery."

Christelle felt much the same way, but she did not mask her feelings with joy. Not that she was an unhappy person, she was just much quieter on the surface.

"I think it is admirable you are able to be happy," Christelle said.

"Do you like it here?" Maili asked.

"I think so," Christelle said. "Everything in my life has changed. I am not as comfortable as you are in Society."

"I am not as comfortable as I appear. I realize what the ladies think of me, and the gentlemen as well. I cannot seem to act with refinement when I am nervous."

Ah. That explained much.

"I also know that none of these men would be paying me any heed if you were not there. I do not have illustrious blue blood running through my veins."

"I would not say that," Christelle said with a frown. "Your parents were gently bred."

"Oh, yes. But it is not the same thing to these people, you see."

"Then why would you want to marry one of them, anyway?" She certainly did not.

Maili traced the outline of the window pane with her finger. "I suppose it is to prove something to myself... that I am as good as they are. But I know what they are saying about me."

For the first time, Christelle felt a connection to Maili. She knew how it felt to be the girl everyone whispered about. She had been that person for six years. It must be a new experience for Maili, and she realized she had misjudged her.

"Catriona told me how it would be. She used it as an excuse to avoid London, but she was in love with John anyway."

"I think you could make a very good marriage, if you wanted to," Christelle said—and she meant it.

"Perhaps. Either way, I choose to enjoy the fairy-tale while it lasts," Maili pronounced with her exuberant self back in place. "Now, I insist you join me for Vauxhall. Even Seamus is coming!" she exclaimed with a giggle.

"Dr. Craig?"

"Yes, can you believe it? He just told me so a few moments ago, in the hall."

Maili twirled herself and her gowns back into her bedroom. Christelle decided to slip away to find Dr. Craig. She had seen him peer into the drawing room earlier and then quickly leave. She could not blame him. She would have liked to escape as well.

She walked through the house, wondering where he could be. She did not wish to enquire of the servants or they might suspect something. Servants knew everything before you knew yourself. That she had learned by being invisible to the others at school.

He was not in the drawing room or the study. She was afraid to try the billiards room, as it would look very odd for her to enter there. Neither would she go to his bedroom.

She frowned and walked out to the terrace. There were a few more minutes before she needed to begin dressing for dinner– something she could do quite well for herself in less than quarter of an hour. However, the family seemed to think she needed an army of servants to attend to her every need.

The gardens were generous for a town house. There was a terrace surrounded by a formal garden, with a fountain at its centre. She kept going beyond the fountain, along the pathway leading to the back wall, where there were trees and a gazebo. The air was heavy and the sky was beginning to darken with the threat of rain. Various flowers were coming into bloom and she inhaled fresh air, feeling a sense of calm overtake her as she stood before the burgeoning rose bushes lining the rear stone wall.

If only she knew what to do. She felt as if she were losing herself. Everyone had grandiose ideas of what they wanted and expected of her, and she had done her best to be that girl. However, Maili's words kept playing through her mind. She could choose.

"I thought I would never find you alone," Dr. Craig said as he appeared before her. She had not heard him approach.

She smiled with joy. "I had to escape," she confessed.

"I do not blame you. You have been quite the sensation, I hear."

His comment wiped the smile from her face.

"I did not mean to upset you. Why the frown?"

Oh, how she wished he would kiss the sadness from her, and take her away from this insanity—even if only momentarily.

"I suppose I am overwhelmed with it all. I have not been used to running non-stop at all hours of the day and night, and conversing with strangers. People I would not choose to converse with under normal circumstances."

He laughed. "It does seem contrary. The *ton* is not a comfortable place if you are not raised to it. Are you enjoying any part of this?"

"Being with my family. I suppose there is some novelty in living in a grand house and dressing like a princess and dancing at balls."

"But they don't make you happy."

"*Non.*"

He understood. Her hand reached out to touch his, which instantly seared her palm. Had he felt it?

She looked up at him. He was everything she wanted in her life. His kindness, gentleness, his humour, his lips…

"Seamus, what is wrong? You have grown quiet," she said as her eyes wandered to his mouth.

"Nothing... I was just thinking of our walks," he replied, swallowing hard.

"Me too." Christelle touched his chin with her fingertips, and she could tell the moment he gave in. He drifted towards her and slanted his lips over hers—gently at first. She leaned in towards him and wrapped her arms around his neck.

Their kiss became more of a gentle dance, exploring and tasting, and she quickly felt her insides warming with an unfamiliar sensation.

He pushed back, and she was already regretting the separation...missing him.

"Forgive me. I became carried away," he said as he put his hand to his brow. "To be seen with you like this would destroy everything."

She reached out to him, but let her hand drop. "What do you mean? Destroy what?" she asked, searching his eyes.

"Your father said several gentleman have asked for permission to court you."

She said nothing. She was not ready to speak of her father.

He shifted uneasily and she heard hesitation in his voice. "I have decided to close my practice here and remove to the country after the Season is ended."

"What?" She turned to stand in front of him and look him in the eye. "I do not understand. Is it not your dream?"

"I am not certain it is. I came to London to find a wife. My few months here have shown me that a family would be neglected if I practice the way I ought. I have a small estate in the country. Perhaps I can find a way to be both a doctor and a gentleman farmer."

He looked up at the sky and she turned back to the roses. He was disturbed by something and she did not wish to upset him further.

"If that is what you wish," she said softly. She began walking away slowly. He would follow if he wanted. He had come for a wife.

He did join her and fell in to step beside her.

"Will you be attending society events then?" she asked.

"Yes, I will begin escorting you and Maili, I suppose, though you have an entourage of chaperones already."

"Funny, is it not, that only a few weeks ago no one noticed if I went about alone with you? And now that my name has changed, I cannot leave the house by myself."

"I imagine the change in circumstances is daunting in more than one way," he remarked.

"Yes, I did not think my father would be so overprotective."

"You must understand it if you see it from his perspective."

"I will do as he wishes." She now sounded like the puppet she felt.

"Will you accept the man he chooses for you?"

Why was he asking her this? Why was he suddenly speaking to her distantly? She longed to beg him to marry her and take her away to the country. But she did not dare. Maybe she had imagined him to reciprocate her feelings.

"He has said nothing to me of him choosing," she answered vaguely, feeling hurt, and as though she could not speak freely to Seamus. It felt as though he had created a wall of awkwardness and she wanted to take a hammer to it.

He looked at her, and she could see he was hurting. But why was he pushing her away?

"Is there something else?" she could not stop herself from asking.

He sighed deeply and looked up at the darkening sky. "Mr. Baker has died."

Christelle gasped and longed to comfort him, to touch him. She took his hand and began to draw circles on his wrist. He watched her for a moment before sighing and pulling it away.

"That is why I was late to your ball. It is also why I have decided to give up my practice."

He turned and walked away, leaving her feeling heartbroken for him and for Mrs. Baker, and longing to run after him.

She did not want him to go to the country and find another woman. She did not care for this marriage market, or the fact that her life was being taken over by people who did not know her. Dr. Craig seemed to understand her, but what else could she do to make him want her? She could tell he responded to her physically, she recalled with a blush, but was she not what he wanted in a wife?

CHAPTER 20

*L*ady Charlotte Stanton, spinster sister of the Duke of Yardley, arrived in time for dinner to meet her new niece. She had decided on accompanying them to the theatre, as *Hamlet* was one of her favourites of the Bard's plays. Christelle had been warned her aunt was quite bookish and eccentric, and she knew she liked her already.

She was rather taken aback when she first saw Lady Charlotte. She looked very much like her father, except not as refined and elegant. She was voluptuous, and Christelle thought if her aunt ever learned that fact, she would have London's gentleman at her feet. She was not as old as Christelle had been led to believe, either, yet Lady Charlotte did not seem to know it. In fact, by her demeanour, Christelle might say her aunt was self-conscious.

The gown of silver satin she wore seemed to accentuate her curves by clinging to her bosom and hips, and Christelle's fingers were itching to draw some sketches for her.

When Lady Charlotte's gaze fell upon Christelle and their eyes met, she exclaimed:

"Oh, heavens! You are a beautiful, feminine version of Benny! I could be very jealous of you!" She came across the room with her arms wide open, and Christelle was afraid she braced herself as she was drawn into the woman's embrace. To her surprise, it felt very good to be wrapped in a familial hug.

Charlotte seemed to realize she had behaved with impropriety as she stepped back and apologized with a sheepish smile.

"There is a reason I had only one Season, Christelle." She laughed heartily. "I never come to London if I can help it, but I will try not to embarrass you. Mama sends her love and begs you to come and visit her for a few days, if you can escape for a while."

"A splendid idea," Yardley concurred, coming across the room to greet his sister with a kiss. "I am certain we will all need a few days in the country before long."

The butler announced dinner, and soon Christelle was caught up in a conversation with Lady Charlotte, who peppered her with questions while ignoring her other dinner partner. Dr. Craig did not seem to mind, but he also seemed more solemn than usual. Christelle did not wish for their relationship to become strained, and she struggled to know what to say.

Immediately after dinner, the theatre party loaded into the carriage and headed for Drury Lane, where they were to meet Sir Anthony Turner and the Duke of Cavenray. For Christelle, the worst part was that everyone seemed to assume Cavenray was courting her, even though few words had been exchanged between them beyond polite trivialities. What was worse still, her father seemed to support and encourage her association with the Duke, when all he had to offer was good looks and a title. She desperately hoped her father knew something she did not. Did he not comprehend that Dr. Craig and Mr. Cole were far more suited to her?

She sat next to Lady Charlotte in the town chariot, facing Dr. Craig and Maili. On any other night, she would have been very excited, but she was still depressed about the way her conversation had ended with Dr. Craig this afternoon. He looked incredibly handsome in his evening ensemble. Tonight he had chosen grey breeches with a silver waistcoat and black jacket, his simple elegance a contrast to the almost frilled look of other gentlemen. Her aunt was very unrefined in a way that was similar to Maili, but Christelle suspected her behaviour would be considered eccentric rather than vulgar in a Duke's sister.

When their carriage pulled up in front of the theatre, the Duke of Cavenray and Sir Anthony were waiting to assist them from the vehicle. Dr. Craig alighted first and helped Maili alight. Then Sir Anthony handed Lady Charlotte down and they seemed quite pleased to see one another, Christelle noticed with some amusement. The Duke, the very same cold fish that Maili had described him as, assisted her descent with a look of approval—if, indeed, he had that much emotion in him.

The crowd parted for them as they made their way inside. It was rather disconcerting. Christelle did not know whether it was for her or the Duke, or the party in general. Lady Charlotte rarely came to town, so it was unlikely she was the cause. Christelle had noticed people tended to move out of her father's way, as well.

The theatre was as elaborate as any ballroom; in fact, more so than any she had seen, which was not many. The party took their seats in the Duke's box, where Christelle sat next to Lady Charlotte, with Maili on her other side. Dr. Craig, the Duke of Cavenray and Sir Anthony sat in the seats to the rear. Christelle quietly took in her surroundings, acutely aware of Dr. Craig in the row of chairs behind her. His musky scent singled him out immediately, only inches from her person. Lady Charlotte and Maili conversed gaily with the others, and Christelle also endeavoured to smile and answer appropriately as she awaited her first play with eager anticipation. The theatre was lined with boxes from floor to ceiling, in a horseshoe shape around the stage. At the front was a pit full of rowdy younger bucks and females who Christelle considered to be loose women by their behaviour and gaudy dress. There were chandeliers suspended from the ceiling, and the curtains and chairs were dressed in rich velvets. The audience was costumed for the evening in bejewelled elegance, and there was a dull roar of chatter while the orchestra tuned their instruments. She was relieved when the curtain lifted and the performers took the stage. Shakespeare had always been a challenge for her to read, as English was not her first language, but the acting was superb and she quickly became engrossed as Bernardo uttered the words, "Who's there?"

When the curtain fell for the intermission, she was rudely and abruptly transported back to London and felt a little irritated when the gaslights were brightened. Everyone around her began chatting again.

"Seamus, would you escort me for a walk to seek some lemonade?" Maili asked.

"Of course. Would any of you like to join us?"

Christelle would have loved to, if she could have been alone with him, but she did not enjoy making her way through crowds.

"I think I will stay," she answered, "but I would welcome some lemonade."

"And I will have champagne," Lady Charlotte said with a merry laugh.

Cavenray followed Seamus and Maili out of the box, and Sir Anthony and Charlotte began a lively discussion about why she avoided London and, therefore, him.

"May I join you for a moment?" Christelle looked up with shock as Mr. Cole took the seat next to her before she could answer. She thought back to her father's words, but she could not ask Mr. Cole to leave without appearing rude. Lady Charlotte did not seem to notice.

"May I say how lovely you look this evening?" he said. "It has been a struggle to keep my eyes on the stage."

She ignored his flattery. "Are you enjoying *Hamlet*, Mr. Cole?"

"I always enjoy a good tale of revenge."

"I would not have thought you bloodthirsty, sir."

"I had not thought so, but perhaps I am. *Revenge his foul and most unnatural murder.* It does make an impression."

"Then why does Hamlet hesitate, if revenge is the answer?" she queried.

"He is a coward."

"Or, in his heart he knows it is more cowardly to seek revenge. His conscience forbids it."

"But look at what happens because of Hamlet's cowardice in delay. How many more people die because of it?"

"I cannot say. I have never seen the play before. But I applaud his discretion in seeking to prove Claudius guilty first. It is unnatural to dwell on the past until it consumes you and makes you bitter."

"I must respectfully disagree, my lady, but I shall say no more and let you decide for yourself."

She smiled and inclined her head.

"Can you truly say you harbour no ill feelings about your past?"

"What good would it do?" And what did he know of her past? Was it common knowledge amongst the entire Town?

"Yes, well, I expect it is a case of all is well that ends well. If all stories had a happy ending, there would be no tragedies."

She thought she detected a hint of cynicism behind his words.

"Indeed. I have been most fortunate."

"I admire your fortitude. It gives me hope for myself."

He stood up as the others returned and left the box. Christelle looked up in time to witness Dr. Craig's reaction to the sight of Mr. Cole. An expression of anger and—dare she flatter herself—jealousy, passed uncharacteristically over his countenance. He masked the look quickly, however, so it was possible she had imagined it. Mr. Cole left promptly after a swift greeting to the others.

"Have a care. Your father would be most displeased," Dr. Craig leaned over and whispered. The touch of his hand on her elbow sent a disconcerting wave of heat through her.

"What was I to do?" she snapped back, a response which drew an elevation of the Duke's eyebrows.

Cavenray troubled himself to lean forward. "Has Dr. Craig been charged with nursery duty?" he whispered in her ear. It had no effect on her at all.

Very likely he had, she mused, but it irritated her that the Duke would point it out to her. She was also annoyed that she had allowed herself to snap at Dr. Craig. Mr. Cole had put her out of sorts.

Turning, she gave His Grace a pasted smile. "He was being a gentleman, sir." Unintentionally, the words came out stiltedly, and in six short words she had defended Dr. Craig and insulted Cavenray. She turned back to face the stage as the next act began, but she saw and heard very little of the remainder of *Hamlet*.

~

What had he let himself in for? Seamus had been repeating the question since the moment he stepped into the carriage to escort the ladies to the theatre last night. Having to watch Cavenray behaving with quiet arrogance as though he already possessed Christelle had been torture enough. To then arrive back at the box to find Cole had sneaked in and occupied her attention for the entire interval was almost enough to break his control. And now, he had been summoned to give a report to Yardley.

He had realized he was little better than a spy, when Christelle had flashed him a look of defiance in response to his reprimand. This would never work.

He rapped lightly on the door to Yardley's study.

"Enter. Ah, there you are, Seamus," the Duke said as he looked up.

Gavin and Lord Harris were also there, along with Yardley's secretary, Hughes.

"You are just in time to hear what Hughes has to say."

Seamus came in and took a seat as the secretary cleared his throat.

"There is very little to report, I'm afraid," the secretary said from behind his desk. "I did verify that Cole has been working for the Foreign Service for some six years. Before that, his history is vague. I could find no record of a gentleman by the name of James Cole, either as a member of Society or as coming from any family with connections. There does not appear to be an obvious relation to the Cole family of Irish Earls of Enniskillen, though the Earl's sister did marry an Englishman. Any offspring would not be styled by his mother's name, of course."

The other four men all frowned, as if contemplating what this information indicated.

"Even if Cole were related, it does not prove any wrong-doing on his part," Gavin concluded after a pause.

"Other than his toad-eating, social-climbing, ungentlemanly behaviour, of course," Harris added with undisguised sarcasm.

"He did manage to catch me unawares last night. He came into the box while I was escorting Maili to fetch lemonade. Lady Charlotte and Sir Anthony remained with Christelle, but she did not send him away," Seamus confessed.

"The blackguard! Although I doubt they have been introduced, and Charlotte would ignore him. I did not think to warn her," Yardley conceded.

"I trust no harm was done in public view, but I shall endeavour not to leave her alone in the future," Seamus said.

"I will speak with Charlotte, should she be the female chaperone again. What say you to our removing to Angelo's? I, for one, could use the exercise. Your father says you are quite the swordsman, Seamus."

"I enjoy it, though I am quite out of practice." He would not mind venting some frustration.

"Then we shall oil the joints today, shall we?" Yardley was saying as they left the room and gathered their hats for the walk to Bond Street.

It felt so strange, Seamus reflected, to be amongst the male scions of his family in this capacity. He was unused to being a true gentleman, by the fact that he had always had an occupation. He still was not certain how he felt about his changed status. Thus far, it had only felt like a stressful family holiday.

They removed their coats, boots and hats, then selected their foils. Seamus was surprised to find how well matched he and the Duke were. His height often gave him an advantage and he would have to hold back with his opponents. It was not so with Yardley. For the first twenty minutes, the only sound was the clash of metal and the movement of feet as they lunged and parried. They entered into the physical battle, with each concentrating on learning the other's strengths. Harris and Gavin were locked in a similar fight on the floor next to them.

They came to a press, their foils crossed.

"Excellent, Seamus! I have not been challenged thus very often." Yardley wiped his brow and took his stance again. "Now you may tell me your opinion of my daughter's suitors," he said as he lunged forward.

"Well, sir, there is quite a court of gentleman following the two ladies."

Yardley was advancing and he had to riposte to regain his ground.

"Yes, I had heard. I suppose it was to be expected."

"It appears as though Cole attaches himself to them in this manner."

"What else do we know of this social mushroom?"

They paused to catch their breath. Gavin and Harris did the same.

"He is being accepted everywhere, though no one knows quite who he is. People are afraid to gainsay him since Yardley accepted him, and he is charming and handsome. At least that is what I heard at the club," Harris said. "I need to see him for myself. I must know him if he travels at all by sea."

"He has an air about him," Seamus said. "And a deuced squirrelly mustachio."

"And a tendency to appear wherever Christelle and Maili are," Yardley sneered.

"Perhaps we shall join them in the park at the fashionable hour today," Harris said, elevating his right eyebrow and narrowing his eyes. He looked dangerous when he did that.

"I have no evidence to support any wrong-doing on his part, but I have a bad feeling about him," Yardley said. He pointed to his chest.

"I just do not like him," Seamus admitted, to the amusement of the others.

"*En garde*," Yardley said with a wide grin.

CHAPTER 21

$\mathcal{C}$hristelle was already growing weary of the Season. Her ennui was made worse by the fact that now she had been granted her wish, and Seamus was close, there was a strange wall erected between them. It must come down. Yet what had built it? Had it been Mr. Baker's death? She could not believe the one she had felt so close to a matter of weeks ago had suddenly changed. Could the death of a patient change a person so? She would have thought a physician might become accustomed to such loss.

It seemed as though she was making everyone else happy except herself. She was playing the part of the perfect lady, but that was not who she really was. She had not been born to be the servant girl she had been for the past six years, either. So, who was she?

Perhaps she was to blame. Perhaps the feelings which had occurred between her and Dr. Craig were no longer possible.

"Would you care for the blue muslin, my lady?" Sybil asked as she held up a walking dress.

"Where are we bound for this time?"

What she would not give for an afternoon of solace, Christelle sighed to herself. She would even scrub the floors if it meant a few hours' respite whereby she might remove the mask of lady and let her hair down.

"I believe you are to enjoy a walk in the park with the sisters and their husbands," the abigail answered.

"Everyone?" Christelle asked with surprise.

"It seems so, my lady."

That gathering alone would be a sight to behold. The sisters had not been feeling well and had refrained from all but necessary engagements.

Sybil helped her into the dress and secured her matching, wide-brimmed bonnet atop her loose curls. Christelle looked at herself in the glass, feeling as though someone else was staring back at her. What had happened to the determined girl who had refused to let the matrons at the school suppress her spirit? She could no longer be that person, but neither could she be precisely who everyone here wanted her to be. She had to reconcile the two... but how?

There was indeed a crowd ready to walk to the park. Christelle wondered if there was a special occasion. Her father and Beaujolais, Lord and Lady Craig, Lord and Lady Harris, as well as Maili and Lady Charlotte, were all waiting.

As they set out, Lady Charlotte took Maili's arm, and Christelle looked about. Perhaps Dr. Craig still had some obligations at the hospital. She was determined to resolve their difficulties today, even if she had to seek him out in his rooms.

Was the discontent she felt because of Dr. Craig? In truth, here she was with falsely elevated hopes she might have a chance to walk on his arm to the park.

"Christelle? Why do you not join us? Seamus is going to meet us there, where you may take his arm."

Maili had read her mind. Her spirits lifted at the news, though it vexed her to know it.

"I wanted to ask you what happened last night? Seamus looked almost angry, though I have never seen him *actually* angry. Was there something wrong with Mr. Cole?"

"I do not know what was wrong. I noticed it as well. Father has taken a dislike to Mr. Cole, but for reasons I cannot fathom," Christelle answered.

Maili wrinkled her face in disbelief. "He seems all that is amiable!"

"I believe it is as simple as the fact he is a stranger—a stranger disguised as a gentleman. It may seem ridiculous to you, but after all your father has been through, he is suspicious of everyone. So, when someone comes into his home uninvited and uses false means to have access to his name and his daughter, he is breaking all the codes of a gentleman," Charlotte said sensibly.

"Mr. Cole purchased a ticket for the stage in Dover on my behalf and helped me to find my way. I cannot think an evil man would do such a thing. I feel indebted to him and cannot cut him," Christelle explained softly.

"That is a difficult situation. I see your point, and I also see your father's," Maili said.

"As do I," Christelle agreed.

"People can be quite brazen when there is personal gain at stake. I think the safest course is to be kind but do not encourage him. Do not put yourself in a compromising situation," Charlotte advised.

"It was what I was attempting to do yesterday evening, before Dr. Craig reprimanded me."

"Did he?" Maili asked, her jaw hanging open in an unladylike fashion. "I can scarce credit it in him!"

"I would not have believed it myself, if I had not heard with my own ears."

"It will be difficult to do anything with the three musketeers watching over your shoulder. I do not believe it is a coincidence that they decided to join us in the park today," Charlotte said.

Maili giggled.

"At least they had the sense to walk, since it is a lovely day. I cannot abide the pomp of bringing a carriage one street in order to go slower than a turtle," Christelle remarked.

They reached the entrance to the park and found most people very willing to exit their vehicles in order to greet them.

Christelle, Maili, and Charlotte were quickly surrounded by a court of Cavenray, Sir Anthony and Lord Weston, but Mr. Cole was not yet to be seen. Neither was Dr. Craig. Christelle tried not to look for him.

She noticed the three musketeers—as Charlotte had coined them —were talking quietly amongst themselves. What were they about?

Out of curiosity, she slowly moved towards them, even though it was shameless to eavesdrop.

"He is most familiar, but I cannot place him at the moment," Lord Harris was saying.

"I cannot agree with Seamus. I find the moustache rather fetching," Lord Craig remarked.

"If only I could see him freshly shaven, perhaps it might come to me." Harris was still pondering, it seemed.

"I might enjoy obliging you on that," her father countered.

Christelle looked up to see the object of their amusement was Mr. Cole, and he was walking directly towards their group. Did the man have a desire to die? She prayed her father would not cut him in front of everyone.

Beyond where Mr. Cole stood, however, was Dr. Craig, and the feeling of warmth she had felt at the theatre rushed over her at the sight of him. It was quickly replaced with a burn of jealousy, caused by seeing him speaking to another woman and observing him smiling down at her. She should look away, but she could not.

"Are you to join our party tomorrow evening?" the Duke of Cavenray asked, as his gaze followed hers to Dr. Craig.

"To Vauxhall? Yes, I believe so," she managed to respond.

"Would that be Dr. Craig, the friendly cousin who squired you about unchaperoned before the revelation?" he asked pointedly, yet still in his lazy drawl.

Her eyes darted to his, and she saw some depth of understanding. He held out his arm to her. "Shall I introduce you to Lady Gordon, whom Dr. Craig is speaking to? She is the widow of the late Colonel Gordon."

As they began to stroll towards Dr. Craig, the sounds of hooves thundering along the carriage way caused everyone's heads to jerk up in alarm. A high-perch phaeton, drawn by matched greys, had shied dramatically away from the crowd and was heading towards the Serpentine at high speed, with a young boy on the box.

Christelle stood watching as Dr. Craig took off after it, being the closest, followed shortly by Yardley, Lord Craig, and Harris. She wanted to scream, but her voice was paralyzed as she watched the horror unfold before her eyes. The lady who Dr. Craig had been speaking to was screaming. The horses were panic-stricken and running at a full gallop, and Dr. Craig's long legs strode to cut them off at an angle as they headed towards him. He went for them with one great leap to grab the reins, and managed to catch hold of something. But his feet were being dragged along and a huge cloud of dust was being stirred up as they neared the Serpentine.

Christelle followed with the mass of people who moved quickly to follow the chase and catch a glimpse of the runaway phaeton. When the crowd arrived, the conveyance had been stopped at the edge of the water, and the horses were helping themselves to a drink. Dr. Craig hurled himself up into the seat and climbed back down with a small boy in his arms.

The boy lay limp in his hold and blood covered his face. His mother was screaming hysterically about her child while Dr. Craig and Lord Craig placed him gently on the ground and began to examine him. Lady Craig tried to comfort her by reassuring her that both men were trained physicians. Yardley and Harris attempted in vain to control the crowds as everyone stared in dread of the feared verdict. Christelle felt helpless.

A few moments later Dr. Craig again picked up the boy and carried him away, presumably to his home. The crowd began to murmur and disperse, but some of their party heard them say the child was still alive, and others were amazed by Dr. Craig's bravery. Their party gathered and walked back to the town house in silence. All Christelle could think was that Seamus was making a mistake in giving up medicine.

~

The women returned to Yardley Court following the eventful walk in the park, as the men escorted the mother and child to their home. Beaujolais had word that the musical evening they were to attend had been cancelled due to an illness. Christelle was not the only one who sighed with relief. She was still trembling from watching Dr. Craig throw himself at the out of control horses and then holding the unconscious boy in his arms.

"A quiet evening at home would be very welcome," Charlotte said as she pulled off her bonnet. Christelle held her tongue and did not point out she had only had to endure a few days of the Season.

"I think we should allow the children to join us, this evening," Beaujolais announced.

"Yes, this afternoon gave us all a fright. It could have been any one of our brood," Anjou agreed.

"I do hope the boy will not come to permanent harm," Margaux said.

"Either way, I will be hearing that poor mother's screams for some time," Maili added.

"Yes, as if Lady Gordon had not been through enough grief to last a lifetime."

"I do hope Seamus is unharmed as well. It was a brave thing he did, but he could have been killed." Charlotte voiced what Christelle was thinking.

"Will the men return soon with word?" she asked.

"I expect Yardley and Harris back soon. They were escorting the mother home while Gavin and Seamus attended to the boy," Beaujolais said.

"We should all rest and settle our nerves for a little while before dinner. Hopefully, they will return by then with good news," Margaux suggested.

"I think hugging my children is in order, as well," Anjou said, beginning to head to the nursery.

The others went their separate ways, but Christelle lingered. Beaujolais stopped and turned to her.

"Forgive me, Christelle. I have not been attentive to you. Do you have a few moments to spare, or would you prefer to rest?"

"You need not feel burdened by me," Christelle said honestly. "I have no expectations."

"But you deserve better. My delicate situation should not be an excuse. I have allowed others to do what I should be doing."

"I have not known any different. With Maili also out this Season, I have hardly been neglected."

Beaujolais sat down. She looked exhausted, and Christelle felt for her.

"But I truly wish to do right by you, and to be your friend. Has any particular gentleman caught your eye? I know your father has said he will not give you up this Season, but he also mentioned Cavenray was paying you marked attention."

Should she be honest?

"He has certainly been much in evidence wherever we are. I am not convinced he is paying me any more mind then Maili, although I suspect it is his way. There is safety in numbers."

Beaujolais laughed. "Yes, he is not overly demonstrative. What of Sir Anthony and Lord Weston? They are often of the court surrounding the two of you."

"Both are very agreeable gentleman," Christelle answered carefully, though her heart longed to shout out that she wanted none other than Dr. Craig. How would the family react?

"But none of them take your fancy, do they?" While Beaujolais asked the question rhetorically, she seemed to assess the situation with considerable accuracy.

Christelle shook her head demurely.

"Fortunately, you will not be pressed to decide. Take your time and enjoy this Season... and please know my door is always open. Always."

"*Merci.*" Christelle smiled.

~

The door closed behind Christelle, and then Lady Ashbury walked into the parlour and took a seat adjacent to her daughter.

"You do realize which way the wind blows, do you not?" She cast a sidelong glance at her daughter.

"Of course I do, and so do my sisters."

"You should have seen them waltz together, *chérie.*"

"A young lady's first waltz always causes her to fall in love with the gentleman. Wait until she has another partner."

"*Non.* I believe her heart is constant. She is different from most girls."

Beaujolais put her hands to her temples. "Could she not choose someone a little more eligible? Someone who at least owns some property with which to house a bride? Not to say that Seamus is not a dear. Perhaps I underestimate his fortune."

"I do not think Christelle cares if she has a house or not. She only wants him. I quite admire her for it, even if it is not sensible."

"Yes, she seems quite determined about him."

"Will you tell Yardley?" Lady Ashbury asked.

"Heavens, no. I do not believe he would appreciate my doing so. Besides, many things can happen in a Season."

"Tut-tut. You are a coward, *ma fille.* There was a time when you relished a heated exchange with your husband."

"But I have learned to choose my battles wisely."

After dinner, the men gathered for a drink in the study. Seamus was sore and exhausted, wanting to retire for the night and partake of a hot bath. But Yardley had asked him to join them. The Gordon boy had slowly regained consciousness, and Seamus and Gavin had left him with his mother, hopeful for a good outcome if he made it through the night.

Seamus had suffered through dinner. He had watched Christelle looking forlorn and toying with her food, desperately wanting to gather her in his arms and declare himself in front of everyone. For some reason, he realized, when a person had experienced a life-threatening event, the fog then lifted and they could see clearly. It was not that he had not known he wanted her or that he loved her, but he had had to do what was best for her. He had determined that he must allow Christelle to have her Season without his interference, believing she might very well change her mind once she came into her own as a Duke's daughter. If not, he would still be in the background, waiting.

He was happy she had found her family, but the selfish side of him felt he had already lost her. He would not be good enough. He knew her father would press for a titled marriage and he understood.

If only they could talk as they had before. It was deuced hard to find five minutes alone with her.

"Cavenray asked me permission to pay his addresses," Yardley announced, bringing Seamus back to the present.

"An excellent match," Harris remarked placidly.

"I told him he would have to convince her. I can find no fault with him, so I gave him my blessing," Yardley informed them thoughtfully over his glass of brandy.

"Quite the recommendation," Gavin mused.

"One could wish he displayed a mite more personality," Yardley conceded.

Seamus almost choked on his drink.

"What of your news, Harris? Have you been able to place Cole?"

"I am confident I have transported him a time or two—although without the queer moustache. I have nothing incriminating to say about him, but I would swear he did not use the name Cole then."

"Keep thinking. As long as the man is hovering around my daughter, I want to know everything about him."

"Has anyone shown any interest in Maili, Gavin?"

"No one has asked for her hand, as yet. Maili is difficult to read. She seems to enjoy the company of whomever is in front of her at the time."

"All will become apparent before long; the Season is still young, yet. At any rate, both girls seem to have taken well."

"With the men, anyway," Harris teased, to the obvious annoyance of his father and Yardley, Seamus noted.

"Lady Gordon seemed quite pleased with you, Seamus. I do hope the boy recovers. There might be some hope for you in that quarter," Yardley remarked.

Seamus looked up from his glass. "Lady Gordon?"

"Did you not recognize she was flirting with you when the boy was off larking with the greys?" Harris added.

"I suppose my mind was elsewhere." He frowned. He had noticed Christelle looking at him—no, glaring at him—while he was talking to the woman. Was that why? The thought filled him with hope.

"She has certainly never talked to me that way—or looked at me with that kind of smile," Harris teased.

"And at her home, after you rescued her son, she was throwing herself at you."

"You merely mistake affection for grief. It is normal for those in shock to attach themselves in such a manner to their trusted physician," Seamus explained.

The men all exchanged glances and burst into laughter.

"What did I say?"

"Poor Seamus. I do think you believe what you just said."

"Aye, it will only get worse, my son. Now you will be a hero in the eyes of the *ton*. Even the King was riding in the park today."

"Our dear Majesty loves to knight people for their heroics. The next thing you know, you will be summoned to kneel before him."

"Now, who is being ridiculous?" Seamus cast his eyes upward.

"Perhaps I should put the notion in his ear. I still owe you a debt," Yardley contemplated.

"Stuff and nonsense, sir. I would beg you be serious."

"Very well, but I will find a way to show you my gratitude one day."

"I did not help her only then to be repaid, and I do not help you now for any reasons other than assisting my family. It has been good to me. It is I who owe a debt of gratitude." Nonetheless, perhaps those things would count in his favour one day.

"You are a true gentleman, Seamus.

CHAPTER 22

*E*ven Christelle was enchanted by the sounds of the evening in Vauxhall. It was a warm night as they rowed along the Thames and summer could almost be smelled in the air. The ladies had dressed with a bit more flair—feeling daring for the whimsical night.

Christelle had selected a flowing floral gown of white with bright tangerine flowers and only a hint of fabric to cover her upper arms. Maili had chosen the gown that shimmered, hoping the fireworks would cause it to shine.

Vauxhall was a beautiful garden, with pathways lined by trees, flowers and hanging lanterns. Water could be heard trickling from fountains and there was soothing music echoing in the background. It was magical indeed. The crowd had come out *en masse* in the warm evening. Christelle had listened half-heartedly to the warnings about all sorts of classes intermingling there. It was part of the novelty, yet part of the danger. She worried not, since she had been part of both classes.

A box had been reserved for their party and they were seated around a table. Waiters quickly served sandwiches of shaved ham, cheesecakes and arrack punch.

Maili had discoursed all day long about which handsome gentleman she could steal a kiss from on one of the dark walks. It did not seem to matter whom, so long as she experienced her first embrace.

Christelle would be very happy with a simple waltz with her preferred gentleman.

Instead, another asked her.

"Lady Christelle, would you do me the honour of waltzing with me?"

It took all of her strength not to look over to Dr. Craig. She smiled kindly at the Duke and took his offered arm, resolving to enjoy herself.

Cavenray took her right hand and placed his left on her back, and she tried to feel sensation from it. He was handsome, after all, and her father approved. Should she try to open her mind?

The music began, and he was eloquent, moving her seamlessly through the steps and twirls without her giving any thought to her own movements.

Surrounded by the scent of floral blossoms, she thought if she closed her eyes she could convince herself she was in heaven. It was the fairy-tale she had dreamed of long ago as she had lain on her bed in the tiny attic room at Harriot's, one where her parents were together and they were a happy family.

Christelle found she was enjoying herself. There was beautiful music, but the dance was…simply a dance. There was not the magic she had felt with Dr. Craig.

She was taken back to the time she had danced with him in the ballroom at Yardley; back to before she had understood what Society was about, and before she had understood about dynastic marriages. When she had fallen in love with her heart.

Society believed love had no place in a marriage. Could she marry this man dancing with her? He treated her well, even if he was a dull conversationalist.

Her heart squeezed painfully at the thought.

185

When the waltz with Cavenray ended, Mr. Cole appeared in front of them before the Duke could return her to the box.

"May I have the next dance?" he asked.

She hesitated. He was behaving in an ungentlemanly fashion again. It really was too bad of him to constantly force her to choose like this. Nevertheless, Cavenray bowed and was walking away before she could make up her mind.

The dance began and Cole took her arm, but instead, he drew her away from the dancing. "I think a stroll on a lovely evening would be just the thing."

"Sir, I cannot leave without informing my parents first." She stopped in protest.

"You will come to no harm on my arm," he assured. "Only a short stroll. I have something important to say to you that requires a modicum of privacy."

"A very short walk, then," she conceded, but when he kept moving farther away from the dancing and her party without speaking, she grew concerned. "Sir, please turn back at once. I must insist!" She planted her feet on the ground, but he kept pulling her forward.

"Do not be gauche. Everyone walks about here. It is what Vauxhall is for."

He was pulling her away without being obvious—that is, if anyone was looking. She considered screaming, but perhaps he was genuine in his need to speak with her. If everyone had not made her so suspicious of him! He was walking and pulling her arm so hard, she could barely keep up. When they reached a small alcove of trees, she grabbed on to a slender trunk and held tight.

"You will force me no further or I will scream. Speak your words now."

~

When Seamus realized Christelle was no longer dancing with Cavenray and had not returned with the Duke, he froze for a split second and panicked before turning and looking about him. It was one advantage of his height. Unfortunately, she was nowhere to be seen. He began to shoulder and elbow his way through the crowds of people. If he was having to do so, he hoped she could not have gone far. He cursed Yardley for putting this mistrust into his mind about a very likely harmless Mr. Cole.

On the other hand, Cole did seem to be a social mushroom and would gain a substantial amount from compromising Lady Christelle. With renewed but controlled panic, Seamus cleared a pathway for himself with zeal. There was a fork in the walk; which way should he go? Surely she would not have gone alone?

He chose the rightward path, but only met with couples locked in embarrassing embraces. He hurried back to the fork and choose the left path.

"Maili!" He found the wrong girl, but the right one all the same.

She giggled, the horrid girl.

He could not see the gentleman whom she was kissing. "Go back and find Yardley, Christelle is missing," he ordered. "I will deal with you later."

He hurried on as he searched for the elusive white dress with tangerine flowers. He realized with horror he was heading toward the gate that led to the river entrance.

Then, he could hear her voice but he could not find her. His worst fears were realized.

"Let go of me, I will not go with you," she was exclaiming. "You tricked me!"

"Yes, I admit to that. How else was I to pry you away from your jailers? You see, there is something you must know and none of them will tell you."

Seamus continued to creep around so he would not be discovered. If he could just find the path to her...he knew he was close.

"I cannot fathom anything so important it warrants an abduction," she said dryly, not hiding her annoyance.

"When you hear what I have to say, you will come willingly."

"Come? I will go nowhere with you. Say what you must, for I imagine my father will not be long in searching for me."

Seamus could hear footsteps coming towards them and was worried Cole would hurt Christelle. He was hoping this would resolve peacefully. He had them in his sights now, but continued to linger, waiting for a safe moment to try and help her.

Cole looked up. He must have heard the footsteps as well.

"You can make this easy or hard. Perhaps we should continue this discussion on the boat."

"I am not leaving with you, Mr. Cole. It is not honourable of you to ask it of me."

"What is honour, precisely?" He scoffed. "The Duchess killed your mother. Was that honourable?"

"No!" Christelle shouted.

"Sweet, delectable Lillian. She was, in her own way, as I imagine you will be."

Seamus was going to strangle the man single-handedly when he got to him.

"Lillian came back to England to beg your father for a second chance. You did not know, did you?"

Christelle was speechless. Could it be true? Either way, it seemed Cole was weakening her.

"I, too, have suffered at their hands. Come with me now and I will tell you the entire story. If you wish to return to them, you may."

Seamus could not wait any longer. He had to make a move. But it was very dark, and it was likely Cole was armed. He could sense the hesitation and surprise in Christelle, and he was very much afraid she would go willingly with Mr. Cole.

Fireworks began to pop loudly in the sky, providing an excellent diversion for Cole. Unfortunately, Seamus thought he saw the gleam of a knife as a brief flash came from one of the explosives overhead.

What game was Cole playing? Why did Lillian's past matter so much to him?

It was now or never. Cole was leading Christelle away towards the gate. Seamus followed behind as closely as he dared, hoping it would be safer when they exited the gardens. He would be easy prey in the cover of the trees. There was also a lady's reputation to protect.

Seamus could hear footsteps approaching and Yardley yelling, "Christelle!"

Apparently he did not care who heard.

"We must leave at once. I do not intend for this to be the finale," Cole growled impatiently.

"I will not leave. I hear my father now."

"Yes, you will." He pulled out the blade and held it to her throat.

Seamus cursed under his breath. It would be better to wait for help. One of them would have to take Cole from behind.

"Why are you doing this to me?" Christelle whimpered.

"You are the unfortunate pawn. When I saw you in Dover, I finally knew how to repay Yardley and his perfect duchess. 'Tis a shame, since I like you."

He pushed her forward and through the gate. Seamus ran after them as Cole forced her into a boat and began rowing away.

"Christelle!" Yardley shouted breathlessly, clutching his side.

"He has taken her by boat!" Seamus called to him.

Seamus quickly scanned the landing and there were no other boats awaiting his convenience. He shed his coat and boots at lightning speed. There was nothing left for him to do but jump.

CHAPTER 23

*W*here are you taking me?" Christelle asked belligerently, as Cole began to row away from the landing.

"Not terribly far. I am only one man rowing. It will not be long before your triumvirate follows. Do not think of jumping. I can throw the knife as well as I can wield it."

Christelle scowled at him. She might take her chances, but she would take them wisely. She glanced about her, searching for any means of escape. The moon was not bright, and the gaslights did not reach this far. The bottom of the Thames would be better than being his captive.

She thought she saw another boat not too far in the distance, and thought she might be able to use it to her advantage.

"Repay my father for what?" she asked calmly, continuing on from his earlier remark, and hoping he would think she was going along with him for now.

He made a sound of disapproval. "Did you learn nothing from *Hamlet*? I had such high hopes for you," he said disparagingly.

"You mean that to avenge his father's death, Hamlet had to commit the very same act for which he sought revenge?"

Cole narrowed his eyes. It gave him a look of the devil. It frightened her.

"I do not understand what this has to do with me."

"Your dear mother and my dear uncle, Christelle."

"Your uncle?" she asked blankly.

"Indeed. Have you any idea what it feels like to be unable to take your rightful place in Society? To be forced to seek employment in foreign lands to hide? To be unable to use your own legitimate title?"

She could hear the venom in his words.

"I do not understand."

"Of course you do not, you have been lied to from the beginning. It is why I decided to save you from them and repay them, all in the same delightful scheme."

"Please enlighten me, then," she said. She noticed the other boat gaining on them from behind. Thankfully, Cole seemed unaware of it.

"With pleasure," he seethed as he pushed and pulled in the oars.

It seemed her chance of escape was becoming possible, but she was also enthralled by what he was saying.

"Because of your father and his Duchess, your mother and my uncle were killed—murdered, to be precise. They spread horrific lies about them and sullied their good names, and therefore my good name."

"Who was your uncle?" She noticed Cole slowed his rowing while he was talking. She must keep him distracted. "Lord Dannon?" she asked as the thought struck her.

"In the flesh." He inclined his head mockingly.

Suddenly, so much made sense.

"Why would anyone condemn you for your uncle's behaviour? Why not prove yourself worthy on your own merit?" Evil must surely run in the blood, she thought. Dannon explained so much... but how had her father seen it?

"You are naive beyond measure," Cole spat. "Are you certain you are Lillian's daughter? She was clever and cunning. Never fear, I have high hopes for you."

"Tell me where we are going," Christelle insisted. Her time was running out. Any moment, Cole would recognize that the other boat was almost upon them. Should she scream first or jump?

"We can have a beautiful partnership. I think you will enjoy your mother's line of work. You must have some of her blood in you."

"Never," she said, seething beneath a calm veneer.

A body sprang up from the river and pulled Cole backwards. He lost his balance, falling into the water, and a terrifying fight broke out.

Oh, she could not watch. But she could not *not* watch. But who was fighting with Cole? The man's back was turned to her, it was dark and they were drenched. It must be her father. She had heard him call out to her.

He threw a punch, and Cole grabbed his opponent around the neck, trying to force him under. Someone from the other boat began yelling at her to come to them, but she could not abandon her rescuer. She took one of the oars, which was much heavier than she would have expected, and reaching out, jabbed Cole in the head. She lost her balance and fell over in the boat.

She heard more splashing and gasping for air and she struggled back to her feet.

She looked up to see that Lord Harris had taken hold of the small craft she was in and was holding out his hand to her.

"Come, Christelle!" he said in hushed tones.

She looked back to the battle in the water and saw there were now three men there fighting.

"Seamus! Father!" she yelled, as one man landed a punch on Cole. They were all going to drown!

Cole was fighting back as one possessed, as if he knew his life depended on it.

"They cannot sustain this for long," Lord Craig was saying.

"Throw them a rope!" Harris ordered to some of his oarsmen. As they were doing so, Christelle saw a flash of metal in the water.

"Look out!" she warned, but Cole's hand was already wielding the knife.

"Nooooo!" a voice yelled as she dived in and joined in the fight, grabbing Cole's arm and holding it tight. She kicked with all her might to stay above the water but her dress worked against her. She could not believe Cole's superhuman strength as she held and bit his arm. He fought like a wild animal struggling for life.

Yardley and Seamus were able to contain him, but swimming while pulling a writhing, kicking beast was difficult.

Christelle could sense one of the men being pulled away and she fought harder to hold Cole's arm as he tried to force the knife down again. They were pushing against each other and the knife was angled down towards her. Her strength would not hold out much longer.

Her father pulled Cole towards the boat, and suddenly she heard the awful sound of metal cutting flesh and Cole stopped fighting.

She was hauled into the boat, and several men dragged Cole in too before lending Yardley a hand. They were all panting and struggling to catch their breath. Her father's arms came around her. "Do not ever do such an idiotic thing again!" he whispered.

But where was Seamus?

"Seamus!" she cried weakly, her voice betraying her. "Where is Seamus?" She looked around, beginning to panic.

"Hush, my love. He was injured. Gavin is tending to him."

She tried to look around the man to find Seamus. She must see him.

Her father held her tight. "Gavin is helping him. You may see him when we are on shore."

The oarsmen were rowing to the bank and it seemed an eternity before they stopped. They must have been at the widest part of the river.

Harris's men lifted Seamus from the boat and set him on the ground. Christelle ran to him and practically threw herself on to him, sobbing.

"*Vous ne pouvez pas mourir!*" she wailed.

"I have no intention of dying, my love," he replied.

She looked up to see two amused eyes twinkling at her.

"You are not dying?"

"I hope not. I might be laid up for a few days, though."

She glanced down at the large makeshift bandage wrapped around his leg.

Her whole body sighed with relief and she took his face in her hands and kissed him, with no regard for who was watching.

A throat cleared loudly. "Christelle."

Seamus pushed her back and she looked up defiantly.

Her father was standing there with a look of dismay on his face. "I had no idea."

She looked up sheepishly, too late remembering they had an audience.

"It is Seamus I wish to marry, Papa."

He was still staring with astonishment.

"If Yardley does not approve your suit after this, I'll call him out myself," Harris said to Seamus as he came to stand over them.

Seamus chuckled before passing out from exhaustion.

~

"For one who chooses to blend in with the scenery, you have made some very big scenes the past two days," Gavin said as he entered the room where Seamus was propped up in bed, much in the invalid state. He vastly preferred the position of issuing commands to that of patient.

Yardley followed Gavin in, looking surprisingly fit after the events of the previous evening. He leaned over to where his daughter sat on the edge of the bed and kissed her cheek, without casting a glance at her. Taking a seat in the armchair next to the bed, he crossed one leg over the other as though it was any typical morning.

"Sir Seamus has quite a ring to it," Yardley teased, languidly examining his fingernails.

"But alas, it is not to be," Gavin said with a grin. He walked to the other side of the bed and removed the bandage, to examine the wound on Seamus's leg.

"Thank heavens," Seamus replied.

"Instead, our King has decided to bequeath you with Dannon's title and lands, which have reverted to the Crown upon Cole's death," Yardley announced.

There was a long, silent pause as the Duke's words registered with Seamus.

"What a ridiculous thing to do for my trying to save the woman I love." *Surely they jested.*

Christelle reached for his hand and squeezed it.

"Face it, my son. You are a hero, and much, much worthier of the honour than Dannon ever was," Gavin said, checking for fever.

"You are serious, then?" In disbelief Seamus looked from one to the other.

"Indeed we are. We have the proclamation right here." Yardley handed it to Seamus, though he did not look at it.

"There is one thing I can agree with Cole on," Seamus said, casting a glance down at his wound.

"And that is?"

"I have no wish to be known by that name."

"A man makes his own name for himself. Although I understand why you would hesitate," Yardley commiserated.

"I am quite content being plain Seamus Craig, you know."

"I know. You are whom I fell in love with," Christelle said with unmasked adoration in her eyes.

"You will still have the opportunity to advance your causes, but now in Parliament. Even more when you add your voice to Gavin's. Think about it. You do not have to decide today."

"The King has not wasted any time." Seamus had barely woken up from his exhausting ordeal. Not only had he swum for what had felt like the length of the Channel, it had been followed up with a fight to the death. It still did not seem real that Cole was gone.

"What I would like to know," Seamus asked Yardley, "is how you managed to have the boat ready? Everything up to that point had been pure speculation on your part. Or is everything truly at your beck and call when you are a duke?" he asked with a grin.

"Not quite. It finally occurred to Harris where he had seen Cole before."

"And where was that?" Christelle asked.

"Jersey."

"I do not remember him from my time there," she said with a frown. "I would have remembered."

"I suspect it was all after you left. He inherited the property upon his uncle's death.

I was also tipped off by Lorena and Noelle, or rather, Beaujolais was."

"The seamstresses?"

"Yes. They were two of the girls we rescued from Jersey all those years ago. Mr. Cole had come there looking for you when he returned to London."

"Oh." The single word was all she could utter. Christelle had not known. "Perhaps they were afraid when they realized I was Lillian's daughter. They were quite different to me after I returned."

"Or they were afraid of Cole."

"Who threw the knife at Cole?" Christelle asked.

The men looked at one another. "I do not know what you are referring to," her father answered blankly.

"Perhaps it is best not to know, my love," Seamus suggested quietly.

"We will leave you two, with the door open," Yardley said, standing up and giving them a warning glance. "Suffice it to say, you have my blessing."

"Thank you, sir." Seamus held out his hand to shake Yardley's.

"I still cannot believe I did not see it before."

"I was trying to allow her to adjust to the changes in her life, and give her the opportunity to change her mind. When one can have a duke or a doctor…"

"Is that what happened?" Christelle asked, clearly offended.

He shrugged a shoulder. "I did not know if I would be acceptable any more."

"Your only charge is to make her happy," Yardley remarked as he and Gavin left the room. Gavin was last to leave and pulled the door shut with a wink.

"I will forgive you for that since you saved my life," Christelle said as she climbed onto the bed next to Seamus and slid her hand in his.

"Very gracious of you," he conceded.

"Seamus?"

"Mmmm?"

"How long were you standing there after Cole took me from the dance?"

"I ran after you the moment Cavenray returned without you. I still cannot believe it."

"How could he have known? Cole had that way of forcing you to do things that were impolite."

"I am glad your father suspected, or the outcome could have been very different."

"Do you think the things Cole said about Father and Beaujolais were true? My heart does not want to believe them, but Lillian was my mother."

"I do not think everything happened the way he portrayed it. He would have said anything to gain your compliance."

"True. Yet I cannot believe Beaujolais was the one to kill my mother."

"I think you need to ask your father and Beaujolais what happened. It will be painful, but they will not withhold the truth from you. It is best you know the entire story."

"It is difficult to think ill of them when they have been so gracious about me, but it is too untenable to know it was her."

"It is hard to see the truth in those we love sometimes. You will have to find it in your heart to forgive her, though it will take some time."

"Seamus, Mr. Cole wanted me to be..."

"Hush. Do not say it. It is time to put that behind us and look to the future."

She nodded as their eyes met and then their lips.

"Please promise me something," she said pulling back just enough to look him in the eye again.

"Anything, my love." Their heads were touching and their fingers were interlaced.

"No more risking your life. Twice in two days is more than anyone should be required to watch."

"I cannot promise. I would do it again in a heartbeat. When I saw him put the knife to your throat, I knew life would not be worth living without you in it."

"You must not say such things, though I feel as you do. The pain would be almost unbearable, but life is always worth living."

"You can die of a broken heart, you know," he retorted.

"But you must not. There is too much good in this world for us to pine over what we cannot change."

"I know you are right, but you are thwarting my best efforts to profess my undying love for you."

"I must be losing my French if I did not realize you were being romantic," she said dryly.

"Hush, my love," he commanded. He narrowed his eyes.

His fingers gently followed the lines of her chin and moved the stray curl behind her ear before tracing the outline of her lips. Seamus leaned forward and gently brushed her lips with his. He leaned back again and looked at her. Her eyes were closed, her face still tilted up for his kiss. Groaning, he leaned in and kissed her again, harder, tasting the sweetness that was everything about his love. It ignited him and he edged closer.

Moving up, he nuzzled behind her ear and slowly worked towards her mouth once more, at first gently and then with more deliberation.

He wanted to tell her how he felt but could not say the words. With his kiss, he tried to say what he had not allowed himself to utter.

Her hands reached behind his neck...tentatively at first. Christelle ran her hands through the back of his hair. Reacting, she moved closer. Seamus pulled away. "Three weeks may be the death of me."

CHAPTER 24

$\mathcal{C}$hristelle was nervous as the familiar bell jingled on the door. She had asked her maid to wait outside.

"Lady Christelle!" Madame Monique called out and walked over to greet her with her arms extended.

Christelle smiled and greeted Madame with a kiss on each cheek. It was very good to see her.

"I have come to see if you may make this wedding gown rather quickly. She held out a sketch of a dress that she had been dreaming of for years. She had never thought the day would come.

"*C'est beau!*" Madame exclaimed.

"It is for my wedding, in just under three weeks' time. Is it possible?"

"Anything for you, my dearest. Dare I ask, is it the handsome Dr. Craig?"

"Yes, there has never been any other."

Madame smiled mischievously. "I knew from the start there was hope."

Christelle's face became solemn. "I know everything now. At least, I know enough. I wish you had told me from the beginning."

"You had enough to worry about at the time. All is well, now?" Madame asked with a sideways glance.

"May we go upstairs? I would also like to see Noelle and Lorena."

Madame nodded and led the way. They sat down and she rang for tea.

Christelle looked around and could not believe how many things had changed in her life in such a short time. She would always be grateful that Madame had taken her in.

After Madame had poured each of them a cup, Christelle finally spoke.

"I suppose it is traitorous to ask this, but I must know, and I do not know who else to ask. Was my mother at fault for what happened? Did she deserve to die?"

"I do not wish to come into the middle of a family matter," the modiste said diplomatically. "I will only say the Duchess had no other choice. Your father would have died if she had not shot Lillian."

Christelle bit down hard on her lower lip. She had not realized Beaujolais was saving her father's life when she had killed her mother.

"It happened here in this shop. Did you know?"

Christelle shook her head and a tear spilled down over her cheek. She inhaled a ragged breath whilst trying to maintain her composure. She had asked, after all. She had known it would be painful, but for some reason, she preferred to hear the story from someone other than her father or Beaujolais.

"And Noelle and Lorena? They were not on Jersey of their own free will?"

"*Non.* Lord Dannon had kidnapped them. There were more girls, but these two chose to come here after they were freed."

"And the others?"

"Some returned to their families. I am not sure about all of them. Your father would know."

"When I was here last, why were the girls cold to me? Have I offended them?"

"You might ask them. I do believe, when Mr. Cole came here

looking for you, they were afraid. They did not want to believe you were in partnership with him, but they did not know what to think."

It was an excruciating realization that her mother had been one thing to her and yet very, very cruel to everyone else.

Madame seemed to understand her thoughts. *"Chérie,* you must be grateful for the time you had with your mother. It was still precious and she helped you become who you are. We may not understand the choices she made, but you are one thing she did right. *Comprenez vous?"*

Christelle could not answer, for her lips trembled and her body shook. Madame held her and let her weep.

Noelle and Lorena arrived when she was drying her eyes, and the fear at once left her as they rushed to embrace her.

"We heard what happened."

"I am very sorry for what my mother has done to you. Is there any way I can make amends?"

"You are not responsible for your mother's actions," Noelle said sweetly.

"I have been eaten up inside since I heard what happened at her hands."

"And it almost happened to you, as well," Lorena said.

"But it did not," Christelle said quietly. "I would be most honoured if you would help me make my wedding gown—and if Madame would allow you to attend the wedding ceremony and the breakfast."

The girls cast each other surprised glances.

They looked to Madame. "But of course." She sent Christelle a look of approval.

"And if you ever find you are ready to set up your own shop in Paris, I would be a most willing silent partner." She looked up mischievously at all of them. "I long to continue designing," she explained.

Noelle and Lorena looked at each other with pleasure and curiosity. "Maybe, one day. We would like that very much. It has always been our dream."

"A dream you deserve to have realized. I must return home for more wedding plans. My father has decided it must be grand," she said with despair.

The girls laughed and embraced her. It felt wonderful to know they could be pleased for her.

~

The Duke could not be talked into a wedding by special license, or out of a grand fête. Seamus seemed to recall Yardley and Beaujolais had been married in a much more demure fashion. Seamus would not protest too much, he was getting his heart's fondest wish. Besides, everyone would be looking at his radiant bride, not him.

St. George's was overflowing with the cream of Society, despite the rainy June day, but there was also a healthy showing of orphans, modistes, and injured veterans. He had to grin. If anyone did look at him, they would think him vulgarly in love with his bride.

They would be correct.

When Yardley and Christelle appeared at the back of the nave, Seamus was comforted by the equally large smile Yardley wore on his own face.

Christelle looked like an angel sent from Heaven. She was dressed in a pale pink silk gown, and the fitted bodice sparkled with thousands of crystals which came to a scallop pattern over her waist. The skirt flowed outward with delicate rows of crystals in a swirling pattern, and he could see her blue slippers peeking out from under her gown, also covered in crystals. A crystal circlet encompassed her golden curls and made her appear the angel she was on the inside.

He himself was much more subtle in his pale golden breeches and coat, but she had ensured he had a pale pink waistcoat to match her dress. He fidgeted with the ring in his pocket, which he had selected for her, and hoped she would like it. He had picked a golden topaz to match her eyes.

By the time the Duke and Christelle reached him at the altar, Yardley's grin was suspiciously beginning to twitch and his eyes looked misted.

"I could not have given her up to any man more worthy."

Seamus swallowed hard. He was going to make him cry. "I will spend every day trying to be deserving of her, sir."

Yardley nodded and placed Christelle's hand in his.

The Reverend began and Seamus scarcely heard a word. He must have answered appropriately for they were announced as man and wife, Lord and Lady Dannon.

Seamus hoped he did not visibly cringe when he heard the name. Until his last breath, he would work to make the title good.

When they had signed the register, they made their way outside to a white carriage decorated with ribbons and bows. The large crowds showered them with flower petals and good cheer as they passed by.

The wedding breakfast was held in the gardens at Yardley Place, which were in full bloom, but every pastel flower imaginable had been brought in to give it an aura of heaven on earth. The rain had stopped and the air was thick with that fresh, earthy smell that only it could bring. Even the sun's rays were cast down from the sky through the canopy of trees and carpet of flowers blessing the happy event.

A faint rainbow could be seen in the distance, and Seamus watched his wife with her new family, still looking as awestruck as the day she had met them. It was a sight to behold. People from all walks of life intermingled here and were accepted here. Christelle was smiling at her friends from Madame Monique's shop and enjoying the feast and the dancing. Children were running around chasing each other with giggles. It seemed everyone had come out to bless their union—Lord and Lady Easton, Lord and Lady Fairmont, Lord and Lady Winslow, and of course, the Dowager Duchess and Lady Charlotte to name a few. Even the Duke of Cavenray had come to grant the couple his best wishes along with the rest of Lady Dannon's mournful suitors. Cavenray was even deigning to dance with Maili, who, for once, did not look thrilled with her partner. She was likely afraid of him, Seamus chuckled to himself.

Servants were passing champagne around and there was a three-tiered cake adorned with flowers made by Mrs. Baker, who had agreed to move to their country estate with them, as their cook.

He looked over to Catriona and John, who he was also attempting to lure from their comfortable home. He and Christelle had decided to make the Edinburgh estate into a laboratory to research plants and their medicinal properties. Seamus would continue to teach as much as he was able with his other duties.

The triplet sisters, even in their *enceinte* state, played a few songs for the party to dance to and enjoy. Rarely did the three of them perform together in public any more, if this could be called public.

Seamus danced with the Duchess, and Christelle with the Duke, in which both participants looked to be crying. Then they enjoyed a lively dance, with Lord Harris for Christelle, and Seamus with Margaux, followed by a dance with her new father-in-law, Lord Craig, who already appeared to love her as his daughter, and he partnered the lovely Anjou. Then, finally, she danced with her beloved. At least he hoped he was her beloved.

It was almost perfect. It was as perfect as it could be and that was more than enough. Even after the rain.

PREVIEW OF RAY OF LIGHT

*T*all, dark and handsome and about as warm as a dead fish. Maili Craig wondered why the Duke of Cavenray had even asked her to dance—a waltz no less—when it seemed he had no intention of attempting even polite civilities. At least he smelled better than a dead fish, she decided as she detected his scent of cloves and spice.

Perhaps if she closed her eyes, she could be more charitable. He did feel very nice and his height was enough not to make her feel like a maypole towering over the other ladies. However, the Duke was the one person she felt most anxious to be near, which was silly since her uncle Yardley was a duke, but something in Cavenray's eyes spoke of disapproval and it put her on the defensive. The knowledge disturbed her, yet she knew it yet could not muster enough grace to overcome it.

Thankfully, he could not detect her sweaty palms beneath her gloves. Under normal circumstances, she would have chatted the dance away as she was prone to let her tongue run on when she was nervous—and she was very, very nervous. This was the first time he had asked her to dance, and she could not fathom why.

Speaking of fish, Maili had felt like a fish out of water without

Christelle along side of her since she had married and departed for Scotland. The Sefton ball was the last entertainment left on the family's social calendar before leaving for the country. The Season had lost its lustre, and the usual court of admirers seemed more reluctant to shower attention on her alone without Christelle present—a lowering thought. Cavenray had frequently been amongst those gentleman seen paying homage Christelle and herself. These last few weeks of the Season had been lonely and Maili feared she had lost her opportunity to make a match.

It was no secret the Duke had been courting Christelle, who had chosen a mere physician—her brother Seamus—instead. To be sure, he was an Earl now, but he had not been when Christelle had fallen in love with him. Maili sighed as she thought longingly about marrying for true love herself. She had dreamed about coming to London and having a Season for as long as she could remember. Her sister, Catriona, had tried to warn her not to get her hopes up or look too high for a husband or she would be disappointed.

Maili had, of course, taken Catriona's words as a challenge.

Maili was dressed as fine as any other lady, she was sponsored by a baroness, a marchioness, and a duchess. She had a smile and charm to put the town to shame, but neither could change the circumstances of her birth. She had been unfortunate enough to be sired by a mere country gentleman.

"Why the sigh, madam? A very longing sigh, it seemed. Would you rather be elsewhere?" the Duke asked breaking the awkward silence at last.

"I beg your pardon, your Grace," she answered demurely.

"I have never before seen you to be at a loss for words."

He had noticed. She could feel her colour rising and felt humiliated. How dare he!

"Please at least humour me and say something so I do not return home feeling as though it was my staid company at fault."

"I never would have thought you, of all people, would seek nor appreciate flattery, your Grace." She almost snapped the words.

"And what, pray tell, do you base this assumption on?" he asked, lifting one haughty eyebrow.

"Your usual silence in my presence," she replied curtly.

"You wound me, Miss Craig." He brought her hand to his heart to feign injury and even proffered a slight, devastatingly handsome smile.

She was not fooled by his too-late attempt to be chivalrous.

"I never intended offence. Most of my thoughts are better left unsaid," he explained.

What Maili would not give to know them. She would be much more comfortable if he would speak and flirt as the other gentleman did. Instead, he always looked at her as though she bore a horn upon her head. She had no witty repartee for him and she hated it.

"Why do you think them better left unsaid? Are they improper?" she asked out of sheer curiosity.

He surprised her by twirling her away from the dance floor, down the terrace steps and to a pathway in the garden away from the revelries of the ball.

"Miss Craig," he began, then cleared his throat.

She waited patiently, though her pulse was racing and her breathing was causing her chest to rise and fall rapidly. She began to fumble with the green ribbon hanging from her gown. Maili looked up to see why he was quiet yet again, only to find him studying her with a dark, hungry look in his eyes.

Was he going to kiss her?

Voices grew closer along the path and he stepped away. She felt an unexpected sense of longing when she could no longer reach him.

"Lord and Lady Brennan," Cavenray greeted the couple coming towards them on the path with a bow. The lady smiled charmingly before dipping into a curtsy. Lord Brennan inclined his head.

"Will you do us the honour of introducing your companion, Cavenray? I have not had the pleasure," Lord Brennan asked.

"Certainly. Lord and Lady Brennan, may I present Miss Craig?"

Maili curtseyed. The lady turned pale as though she had seen a ghost and grasped her husband with both hands. "Margaret?"

"No, my lady," Maili responded at once. "My mother was Margaret. Did you know her?"

"But you are dead!" Lady Brennan exclaimed, holding a hand over her mouth in obvious shock.

AFTERWORD

Author's note: British spellings and grammar have been used in an effort to reflect what would have been done in the time period in which the novels are set. While I realize all words may not be exact, I hope you can appreciate the differences and effort made to be historically accurate while attempting to retain readability for the modern audience.

Thank you for reading *After the Rain.* I hope you enjoyed it. If you did, please help other readers find this book:

1. This ebook is lendable, so send it to a friend who you think might like it so she or he can discover me, too.
2. Help other people find this book by writing a review.
3. Sign up for my new releases at www.Elizabethjohnsauthor.com, so you can find out about the next book as soon as it's available.
4. Come like my Facebook page

www.facebook.com/Elizabethjohnsauthor or follow on
Twitter @Ejohnsauthor or write to me at
elizabethjohnsauthor@gmail.com

ACKNOWLEDGMENTS

There are many, many people who have contributed to making my books possible.

My family, who deals with the idiosyncrasies of a writer's life that do not fit into a 9 to 5 work day.

Dad, who reads every single version before and after anyone else—that alone qualifies him for sainthood.

Wilette, who takes my visions and interprets them, making them into works of art people open in the first place.

Karen, Tina, Staci, Judy, Shae and Kristiann who care about my stories enough to help me shape them before everyone else sees them.

Tessa and Heather who help me say what I mean to!

And to the readers who make all of this possible.

I am forever grateful to you all.

ABOUT THE AUTHOR

Like many writers, Elizabeth Johns was first an avid reader, though she was a reluctant convert. It was Jane Austen's clever wit and unique turn of phrase that hooked Johns when she was 'forced' to read Pride and Prejudice for a school assignment. She began writing when she ran out of her favourite author's books and decided to try her hand at crafting a Regency romance novel. Her journey into publishing began with the release of Surrender the Past, book one of the Loring-Abbott Series. Johns makes no pretensions to Austen's wit, but hopes readers will perhaps laugh and find some enjoyment in her writing.

Johns attributes much of her inspiration to her mother, a former English teacher. During their last summer together, Johns would sit on the porch swing and read her stories to her mother, who encouraged her to continue writing. Busy with multiple careers, including a professional job in the medical field, writing and mother of small children, Johns squeezes in time for reading whenever possible.

ALSO BY ELIZABETH JOHNS

Surrender the Past

Seasons of Change

Seeking Redemption

Shadows of Doubt

Second Dance

Through the Fire

Melting the Ice

With the Wind

First Impressions

Out of the Darkness

30885566R00136

Made in the USA
San Bernardino, CA
31 March 2019